Four and a half Kisses!

"For readers wanting both heat and sweet, Leigh Ellwood hits all the right notes in her erotic romance, **Truth or Dare**. Ms. Ellwood's characters are engaging, her writing style is lively with a touch of humor, and her sex scenes sizzle."

—*Romance Divas*

Four Stars!

"Truth or Dare is both a love story and a journey of discovery. I was privileged enough to have a ringside seat on this voyage."

—*Just Erotic Romance Reviews*

Four Hearts!

"This book will definitely keep you on your toes with all of the interesting twists and turns."

—*The Romance Studio*

TRUTH or DARE

An erotic romance novel by

LEIGH ELLWOOD

PHAZE

Cincinnati, Ohio

PHAZE

6470A Glenway Avenue, #109
Cincinnati, OH 45211-5222

Paperback ISBN 1-59426-511-9

Truth or Dare © 2004 by Leigh Ellwood

Cover art © 2004 by Stacey L. King

Phaze is an imprint of Mundania Press, LLC.

This is an explicit erotic novel intended for the enjoyment of adult readers. Please keep out of the hands of children.

PROLOGUE

"Hello?"

"What are you wearing?"

"Who is this?"

"You got on those black bikini panties I like so much? The ones you were wearing at the Tavern when I dropped my fork and had to go under the table to get it?"

"What the fuck—Brady?"

"Nice to know you're not screening all your calls."

"This connection is terrible. Are you still in Europe?"

"I'm in a cab, heading home. I got in an hour ago, not counting what I spent in line getting through customs."

"Yeah? Well, welcome home. Did you have a good time?"

"Yeah, I did. Would've enjoyed it more if I had some company."

"Brady, don't—"

"Claire. Come on. You know, I was kind of hoping for a warmer welcome than this."

"Brady. Jeez, you know everything I had to say I said before you took off."

"And nothing's changed? Absence hasn't made the heart grow fonder?"

"Nothing's changed. I'm sorry."

"I spent a lot of nights alone."

"Don't."

"Thinking about you, wishing you were lying next to me, underneath me."

"Stop it. You're only making it worse for yourself."

"Thinking about your bare skin pressed next to mine—"

"I'm going to hang up if you don't stop."

"I just want to bury my face in those beautiful tits of yours."

"I mean it."

"I mean it, too. I'm not looking forward to going home to an empty bed."

"Brady, how many times do I have to tell you? It's not going to work out between us. We just don't mesh."

"Funny, I thought we meshed fine."

"It's more than just sex, Brady. I just don't think we're compatible; our backgrounds and interests are different. I told you that."

"And I told you that you didn't give us long to really find that out."

"Yeah, and what do you do? You leave the country."

"You could have come with me, you know that."

"You know I can't just take off on a whim, Brady. I work."

"And I don't?"

"It's different. *We're different.* That's why it can't work. You need to grow up."

8

"Claire…"

"What?"

"Can I come by? We can just go out for a drink. I promise I'll behave and I won't drop any forks…"

"I don't think that's a good idea."

"Why not? It's early yet."

"Brady, I can't. I, uh…"

"You, uh. You have plans?"

"Yes."

"Okay, then. Can I call you later, then? Are you going to be answering your phone instead of screening numbers, one hopes?"

"Don't, Brady. Don't torture yourself. Look, I have to go. You take care of yourself, okay?"

"Claire, just wait a sec. Claire?"

ONE

"Claire, damn it, pick up. I know you're there," Brady Garriston muttered into the receiver as the muffled ring tone hummed in his ear. Two rings, three rings, four rings, *click*. Now there was static on the other line, followed by a benign recording of Claire Walker's voice telling Brady to leave a message and that she would get back to him as soon as possible.

Frustrated, he placed the receiver back against the wall. She was either screening her calls or she really had gone out like she said she was planning. Either way, he had to accept it—it was over. He sighed.

He let his eyes wander to the kitchen counter, where he noticed a small mountain of unopened mail about to slide into the sink. He laughed softly at the pending avalanche; his daughter Melissa, a student at NYU who lived with friends in the Village, had been instructed only to take with her the bills and any other important documents arriving at his apartment during his absence. This left him apparently with dozens of notices declaring that he may have just won a million dollars.

Sorry Mr. Clark, Mr. McMahon, he thought to himself, *that I wasn't here to collect, assuming you stopped by with a gigantic novelty check in my name. Better luck next time.*

His ex-wife had called him foolish, allowing his daughter free rein over his checking account and access to his apartment while he dawdled around Europe and basked in the magnificence of cultures long dead, feeling sorry for himself. "Just don't be surprised when you come back and discover you only have seventeen cents in the bank," she warned. "It won't take much for her to plow through the Garment District."

"How can I be sure you wouldn't try the same thing if I asked *you* to handle my expenses?" he had asked her slyly over the phone the night before boarding the plane. "I think I can trust my own flesh and blood with this."

"Don't be too sure," a singsong reply caressed Brady's ear. "She just might take revenge, considering you aren't taking her to Europe with you."

Brady sighed as the memories faded into white noise, and he plunged his hands into the junk mail pile, sifting half-heartedly through it. He looked at his watch. Nine-fifteen at night on a Friday—New York City was just waking up for the night, eager to revel in varying degrees of merriment and debauchery after eight hours of clock-watching. Messages retrieved on his cell phone revealed that he had no offers for projects and bookings waiting for him, either, and no prospects of any in the near future. His ex-wife was happily married to an orthodontist in Connecticut, his little girl was grown and preoccupied with her own life, Claire was moving on without him, and he was alone.

"Great," he whispered involuntarily, dropping the mail back on the counter and retreating with the last of his travel bags to his bedroom. He tried not to feel bitter about it. Claire did deserve a real boyfriend, somebody strong and self-sufficient, and she had said she wanted as much. She wanted somebody dependable, and apparently a dependable man was not the type to jet across country on a whim.

But what was wrong with being spontaneous, being fun? Surely lawyers were permitted to cut loose every once in a while.

"I'm not an idiot," he said aloud, staring balefully at the array of luggage he had tossed on his bed. Yes, he was famous, and had money, and liked to spend it and do wild things. He had earned the right to do just that. Why did Claire have to equate a fun-loving attitude with immaturity? Angrily he poked at a bag. Who had rammed that stick so far up her ass?

He sighed. Such a nice, heart-shaped ass it was, too. What he wouldn't do for a nice piece of ass right about now. To think, too, he had behaved himself in Europe. He didn't take advantage to get to know of any of the pretty girls floating past him on Paris streets, or lounging in Venetian gondolas, or leaning over a rail in Rome for a better view of stone ruins, supple breasts in full view and threatening to spill from a floral sundress.

Instead, he had made good use of his right hand for much of the trip. It certainly would not have done his career any good to let his lust take over his senses, leaving him to slut all over

Europe. They had gossip tabloids, too, and his records sold well over there. No sense in endangering his career to satisfy his lust.

Brady rummaged through folded shirts and pants, forcing a chuckle. What career, he had to ask himself. He·had not cut an album in almost two years, and while the royalties on his previous works were still brisk, he knew he could not live on them forever. The well would eventually run dry if he continued to spend and did not become productive again.

He froze. This was probably what Claire had meant by his being immature. Quickly, though, he shook his head and resumed. He was spontaneous, yes, but never careless with his money. He had hoped the trip would inspire him to write some new material. Instead, he arrived home with an armload of dirty laundry and empty notebooks.

Yet the trip was not a total loss. He smiled, thinking back to the pretty scenery of Europe, particularly that of the feminine persuasion. God, but was he horny right now. His cock stiffened slightly. Why couldn't Claire have changed her mind about him when he got back?

He tossed his dirty clothes on the floor. No visitors were expected, no photo shoots for *People* or *Rolling Stone* were booked, so who was going to see how slovenly he lived? Who was going to care?

He felt tired, but not so fatigued as to want to sleep. There was so much to do now. He wanted to write again, record again.

He wanted more of a homecoming than an

empty apartment, too. It would have been nice to have somebody welcomed him home by wrapping her legs around his waist as his cock firmly imbedded itself in her pussy.

There was that feeling again, however, that hardening in his pants that required a woman's touch to appease. Now, though, it would have to be his own, just for the sake of ending it.

"God, help me."

A fleeting thought of retirement flashed through his mind. He shook the notion away with the cobwebs, removing his stale shirt and unbuckling his belt as he padded into the bathroom. The Stones were nowhere close to retiring, and The Who were always coming *out* of retirement. Those guys were older than he was. Why should he consider hanging it up because of writer's block? Could he afford to now?

I'll get over it. I'll be fine. He had endured many lows professionally and romantically, and survived.

I'd feel much finer after a blowjob, though. He sighed.

He caught his face in his bathroom mirror, and nearly panicked at the sight of the stranger before him. Whose face was this? Who owned these hollow, gray eyes—eyes a national celebrity magazine had once called haunting and, coupled with his silky bass, able to bring a woman to climax—sinking underneath worried brows? His dark brown hair, cropped closely to his head, showed threats of silver, especially around the temples and sideburns. Loose jowls and bags under his eyes were evident in the harsh light lining the mirror.

No wonder he was able to slip through La Guardia unrecognized—he looked terrible. Even in the city, where television and movie personalities could roam unfettered, Brady averaged about ten autograph requests a day while strolling along the streets. Here, he looked old, nothing like the suave Lothario who had graced his album covers over the past twenty-five years.

Momentarily he pressed his forefingers above his cheekbones and pushed the skin backward, smoothing away the wrinkles. It was hardly an improvement. Other performers, either friends or acquaintances, had succumbed to the knife in order to keep up with the legion of pre-packaged boy bands vying for their audiences. While not a vain man, the thought of a slight nip and tuck had crossed Brady's mind on occasion, but the end decision was always the same. Improving his looks was secondary to improving his craft, which needed all the help it could get right now. At least his face did not look like it was going to melt.

I'll embrace gravity, thank you, he silently told the mirror, and released his touch. Wasn't fifty supposed to be the new thirty, anyway? Weren't men supposed to get sexier as they got older, like Sean Connery and Harrison Ford? Had they succumbed to the knife? Regardless, he would remain untouched. To try to recapture youth in such a way would be...

Immature.

He removed his clothes. At least the rest of

his body did not show the ravages of time as well. Consistent diet and exercise left his body well-toned and easy on any woman's eye. His blessedly large non-musical instrument proved no need for artificial stimulants, if his current, growing state of arousal was any proof.

In the claustrophobic confines of his tiled shower stall, Brady let the stinging hot water wash away the grime and muscular discomfort of the long transatlantic flight home. Finding a sliver of bay-scented soap resting in its cove, he lathered his chest and arms, trying to ignore his growing erection.

Fat chance. It would not be ignored, and no-body was going to slip into the shower to help.

He closed his eyes and arched his face into the spray. His right hand, still palming the soap, slid down his abdomen to rake through the patch of damp pubic hair covering the base of his now erect cock. Brady cupped his swollen scrotum, caressing the growing ache, and worked his hand slowly up and down his shaft, squeezing his circumcised tip and tracing the bobbing veins. His left hand idly plucked at one nipple, already puckered from the water needles stabbing his chest, then the other. Oh, to have somebody—anybody, Claire, whoever—in here with him to do this. Just to feel a warm body clinging tightly to his.

Here, now, there was only the water to cover him as the buildup of his emotions burst, and he came, shooting his load into the tile with a stifled cry. His orgasm was quick but racked his entire body, and it dissolved quickly as he opened his eyes to see what was left of the soap spiraling with his come into the drain between his feet.

He looked at his hand, wrinkled from prolonged exposure in the shower. If it wrinkled any more, perhaps it would atrophy. He wouldn't be able to play piano if he kept this up, he realized.

Mute, he quickly rinsed, then ceased the shower's flow with one strong yank on the faucet. He toweled himself off, cinched tightly his terry cloth robe, and shaved. His appearance improved as a result, but not so his mood, the one-armed exercise in the shower notwithstanding.

As he applied a cold, stinging after-shave to his face the bedroom phone rang, jarring all melancholy thoughts to the back burner.

His heart leaped into his mouth. *Claire?* Had she changed her mind after all?

The robe's belt loosened as he dashed out of the bathroom, causing the flaps to fly wide open and expose his skin to the cold. Goose flesh erupted on his legs and hips; unconsciously one hand fell to rub it all away.

He answered on the second peal, then tried to mask his disappointment as he greeted the caller.

"The Prodigal Son of a Bitch returns!" hailed the hearty voice on the other line. "You better have brought me back something nice."

Brady smiled, happy to hear Cal Briscoe, his best friend and one of the best studio musicians in the city. He returned the greeting in the cheeriest voice he could muster. "I tried, but she wouldn't get into the suitcase," he joked. "I'm guessing a little bird named Melissa told you I was back?"

"Bingo. She said she figured you could stand to see some familiar faces again, you know, to get back in sync," Cal said. "Now, granted, I probably ain't as appealing as those French broads you probably met overseas, but I was just finishing up here—"

"Where's here?" A pang seized his chest. He listened closely and heard laughter in the background on Cal's end.

"Sound on Sound." Cal mentioned one of the many recording studios in the city. "Chelsea's calling it quits for the night. I've been here since six."

Brady nodded. Of course Cal would be working, there was no reason for him to wait around for Brady to decide to record again. Chelsea, being a popular jazz vocalist, would certainly want the best bass player on the eastern seaboard, if not the whole country, to accompany her deep, honey-coated vocals.

"I thought I'd head out to Knickerbocker's to get a bite," Cal was saying. "Why don't you meet me there? You could regale me with stories of near misses from driving on the wrong side of the road."

"Chelsea's busy then, huh?" Brady teased. It was common knowledge among those in the music industry that the jazz diva tended to engage in more than professional relationships with her musicians.

"Drummer beat me to her, no pun intended."

"Okay, sure, Knick's is fine," he chuckled. "It'd be nice to have a cold, watered-down American beer again." He tried not to sound too lacking of enthusiasm. It would be nice to see Cal again after such a long absence, but in truth he did not feel hungry. Actually, he was hungry, but not for one of Knickerbocker's signature hamburgers.

His cock stirred again.

Stop it, he admonished himself. He was going mad. "I'll see you down there in, say, half an hour?" he told Cal.

Cal affirmed and Brady hung up the phone. Yes, he decided. Maybe not something to eat, but a drink would be good, anyway. A drink might help him forget his problems, if only momentarily.

He looked down at himself, willing away another threatening erection.

Europe had not done the trick. He wondered if anything would.

.

TWO

"He's back? Are you sure? Oh, hold on for a sec. I can't hear you for *CSI*."

Ellie Shaw snatched an unruly lock of her long, blond hair and packed it firmly behind her left ear. With her other hand, she smoothed the expanse of beige sofa to her right and grasped the remote control, easing her yawning Persian, Typhoid, onto the carpet in the process. Pressing a button immediately muted the explosive argument between the televised crime scene investigators, and Ellie retrieved the handheld phone from her lap to resume the conversation.

"Did he call you?" Ellie demanded of her cousin, not skipping a beat.

"Yeah, I just got off the phone with him," sighed Claire Walker on the other end. "You know how I screen all my incoming calls with Caller ID—"

"You better. No single woman living in New York City needs to be answering her phone with all those pervs on every street corner. I'm glad you finally moved into that new building, too." Ellie was emphatic, and cast a worried glance over her shoulder to confirm that her own door was securely locked. Dareville, Virginia, while not the perpetually humming metropolis New York City was, also had the potential to produce a lunatic or two. It just had yet to do so, but that meant nothing to Ellie. There was a first time for everything.

Fleetingly Ellie hoped, if any lunatics were prowling the neighborhood tonight, that the large dog bowl marked for an imaginary canine named Butch that she kept on the back porch by the sliding glass door would prompt them to think twice before breaking into her garden apartment. Then she shook her head and giggled. She was watching way too many cop shows.

"What's so funny?" Claire wanted to know.

"Hm? Oh, not you," Ellie said gaily. "I'm just letting my imagination take over again. I should really switch to the Food Network. So, he called but you screen the numbers and answered anyway?"

"I was expecting somebody else and didn't check this time, that's how I got stuck talking to him," Claire said. "I didn't think he'd be back so soon."

"So soon? He was gone for a few months, wasn't he? How long were you expecting him to stay over there?" Ellie squeezed her eyes shut to conjure the memory of an article on Brady Garriston she had read in an old entertainment magazine she found at the library. Ellie had not owned a Brady Garriston album in her youth, and had known very little of his music at all. Yet, the day her cousin had revealed to her that she was dating the star, Ellie plunged headfirst into a crash course, researching him on the Internet and through a CD store on her last trip to Virginia Beach. She had not realized before how good his music was.

In the event Claire decided to one day introduce the two—and surely Claire would want the famous love of her life to meet a woman who was more of a sister than a cousin—Ellie did not want to appear too fawning, but did not want to look ignorant, either. The next words out of Claire's mouth, however, made her feel foolish.

"I don't know, I didn't give it much thought," Claire said. "It's over. We have nothing in common. He's like a big kid, and he doesn't want to grow up. The fact that he took off for Europe the morning after I dumped him should say something about his flighty behavior."

"Pun pardoned," Ellie murmured with a smirk.

Claire continued as if she had not heard her cousin. "You break up with some men, they'll go to a bar and drink away their sorrows. A bar *down the street*, not a thousand miles away. He can't do anything normal. He's just not for me."

"I don't get you, Claire. What's wrong with acting like a kid at times?" Ellie unfolded herself from the sofa, wincing as her bare left foot tingled back to life. She stomped it on the carpet and limped to her galley kitchen. "I mean, I'd think it romantic that a guy would be so upset that he would go to such lengths to heal after I dumped him. And you don't know if he drank himself silly in some English pub." Give her a man with wanderlust over an alcoholic any day.

"You know, I *might* have given him some credit if he had gone somewhere for a week, like the Adirondacks or even LA. But flying to the other side of the planet? That's just so weird, you know?" Claire laughed woodenly. "Who does that?"

"It's not *that* far. Not like he went to Tibet to meditate on a mountain." Of course, that sounded even more romantic than Europe, but Ellie dared not mention that.

Ellie fished through her packed freezer, moving aside marked, plastic containers of tomato sauce and soup until she found the pint of chocolate chip ice cream. Many questions bubbled in her mind. Why would Claire so easily distance herself from a guy who sounded so sweet and, from what Claire had divulged in the past, was obviously smitten with her? And when had Claire suddenly become such a fuddy-duddy about men? Law school had to have done this to her. Ellie could recall a few of Claire's past boyfriends who seemed as equally wild as the famous Brady Garriston, if not wilder.

"What's the harm in seeing him again, for a drink?" she suggested. "From what you're saying, it's obvious he's not over you. Yeah, he didn't call while he was away, but maybe he was just giving you time. That's a rather mature thing to do, you think?"

"I don't know, El." Claire sounded wary. "He's fifty years old—almost *twenty years* older than we are—and he acts like a teenager. He is a great guy, but he's not the guy for me."

Ellie plunged a spoon into the thick, melting cream, feeling immediately contrite. He was not a serial killer, for crying out loud. Claire could do worse. "Yeah," she said. "Whatever."

"And I'm sure tonight's phone call and offer of an innocent drink was nothing more than an attempt to get me in the sack again."

Ellie's skin prickled at this. Claire had not mentioned before that she and Brady—that she had been with a *bona fide* rock star! Suddenly an image of her Prada-wearing cousin tarted up like a groupie—Spandex and plastic bangles and gaudy makeup—burned in her mind. She had heard stories of the many sexual exploits of musicians while on the road, but never considered her straight-laced cousin might become a statistic. True, Claire was not exactly pure as the driven snow, but Ellie knew she took her sex in small, easy to handle doses.

Yeah, she had heard about rock stars, too. One of her favorite entertainment magazines included a column for "blind items," anonymous gossip contributed by people who claimed to have scored with certain celebrities, leaving no detail untold except for names. She wondered about Brady Garriston. Was he as skilled with his personal "equipment" as he was with a musical instrument? Had he ever been implied in one of those blind items?

Unconsciously she pressed the frosted pint container against her breast. The fabric of her sleeping T-shirt was worn thin from numerous washings, and as the container slid across her chest, one nipple immediately hardened. Unbidden, then, came an image of her cousin writhing in bed underneath Brady Garriston, spread-eagled and moaning with delight with every stroke of a large, rock-star quality cock inside her.

She wondered if Claire would be so brazen as to contribute to that blind item column herself. She moved the container to press against her other breast. Soon she was going to have it move it further south to cool down, she realized.

Stop it, Ellie berated herself. Once again, her imagination had seized her better judgment and was taking it on a joy ride.

"What will you do if he calls again?" Ellie asked her finally. She wondered if Claire had realized her slip.

Claire sighed. Ellie heard a refrigerator being opened on the other end. She knew her cousin was reaching for her own favorite medicine: rocky road. "Nothing, I just won't answer it," Claire said finally. "I don't think he'll call back anyway. He'll find somebody more suited to him. He deserves a great gal, I'm just not the one."

Ellie slumped against her closed refrigerator, with the receiver pinned to her shoulder as she plowed a curling trail through her own pint carton. Hardened bits of chocolate caused her spoon to snag, so she settled for a smaller bite than anticipated. A muffled mewling sound signaled Typhoid's presence in the kitchen, and Ellie watched the cat lovingly curl around her ankles. When Ellie made no move to share her treat, the cat just as quickly trotted away.

"I'm sorry, Claire," she said, a bit guilty for feeling more sorry for herself. To live vicariously through Claire meant having to weather the disappointments, and she was truly disappointed this thing with Brady Garriston did not work out for her cousin. "I hope everything works out for you."

"It will." Claire sounded better now, talking through a mouthful of ice cream. "Starting tonight. I got a date with a really nice guy. He's a stockbroker, works three floors above our offices."

Ellie rolled her eyes. A stockbroker. Let the good times roll. "Sounds like fun. Make sure you bring a book to read."

"Ooh!" Ellie heard a spoon clatter against a hard surface, then hurried movement. "He's gonna be here in fifteen minutes, and I'm not ready," Claire said. "Can't believe we've been talking this long."

"Fifteen minutes?" It was nearly eleven. Ellie's favorite show had just ended; she had missed learning the identity of the criminal of the week. Now she would have to wait for a rerun or for the show to be released on DVD. "You're going out *this* late?" On a *weeknight*?"

She was answered by patronizing laughter. "El, it's New York. Unlike Dareville, this town doesn't shut down at sunset."

"You know damn well we do not shut down early," Ellie countered, "we just..." There was no point, however, in arguing with Claire. Dareville might as well have been situated in the darkest jungle of South America with only one indoor bathroom for the entire population, for all her city cousin thought of their hometown. True, the hamlet of three hundred—give or take—did not have the glamour and power of New York City, or even nearby Virginia Beach, but it suited Ellie fine, hence she returned after college while Claire fled at the first opportunity. Ellie lived very well on her teacher's salary, and anything she could not readily find in the antiquated town square could be bought in Virginia Beach or via the Internet, which could be accessed in Dareville. Trappings of the twenty-first century in Backwater, USA. Imagine that.

With a heavy heart she wished her now excited cousin a good evening and disconnected, shoving the pint back into the freezer. Already she could feel the fat solidifying on her thighs.

Her show had segued to the Norfolk/Virginia Beach news, which did not interest her. Curled in one corner of the sofa, Typhoid now snoozing at her feet, Ellie shut off the set and leaned back against the throw pillows, momentarily closing her eyes. The temptation to rise from her comfortable position to put on a CD passed; after a day of educating twenty second-grade students, the quiet of her apartment was a blessing.

Still, it would be nice to live a little, stay out past midnight on a date with a handsome man. At this point, even a dull stockbroker seemed like a prize.

A handsome rock star would better fill the bill. Yeah, Brady Garriston was fifty-something, but Ellie had to admit the guy was *fine*.

A smile played on her lips as she touched her chin; a streak of white cream had lingered there and she dipped her tongue over her lower lip to lick it away. She stretched quietly, working out the kinks in her legs and neck, and lay back on the couch, resting her folded hands against her abdomen. The fantasy she had nursed for the entire time Claire and Brady dated returned vividly, and flickered through her mind like a film as she closed her eyes.

Ellie saw herself being introduced to the famous Brady Garriston, a timid offer of a handshake on her part fast becoming a warm, familial hug. Of course, even a star like Brady would be more than cordial to Claire's beloved cousin; he would want Ellie to like him, to approve of him.

She imagined the warmth of his body against hers, his hands gently caressing her back. It had been so long since a man had touched her so intimately. She could feel all that ice cream she had consumed melting into a sizzling pool inside her.

Unconsciously a hand came to her breast, and she plucked at her nipple though the thin fabric. Yes, Claire would have introduced the two if they had stayed together, and Brady would have drawn Ellie close, so close that Ellie would feel the bulge in his crotch pressing between her thighs.

Claire's told me so much about you, Ellie. I feel like I know you so well, that deep voice would buzz in her ear, making her wet.

Ellie closed her eyes. Her other hand snaked down her side, pulled up the hem of her shirt, and slid underneath the elastic band of her now soaked panties. She inhaled an imagined scent of masculine cologne, her skin flushed with the imagined contact of Brady Garriston's lips brushing against her ear, his hands trailing from her shoulder blades to her backside. And Claire's distant voice, mentioning something about having to leave the room and get the luggage out of the rental car...leaving them alone.

Her fingers slid through her cleft and down to her clit, which she started to rub in a circular motion.

I was wondering, Ellie, if you could help me out for a second. You see, I've been thinking of giving Claire something, to show how much I care for her...

She pictured Brady pulling away only slightly to undo his jeans, releasing the impressive package within its confines. Her movement on her clit increased, along with the sensation that sent ripples of delight washing over her. Yes, Brady Garriston would *have* to have a rock star quality-size cock. The kind cast in plaster by some groupie for posterity. It had to have been part of the job description to have a big dick.

I'm not sure it would fit Claire, you know? It might be too big for her to handle. And, since you two are about alike, I was wondering...

There came another movement, this one from the far arm of the couch. Ellie sat up with a yelp, her heart thudding against her chest as Typhoid mewed a greeting and slinked closer to snuggle against her shoulder. Ellie let out a loud, frustrated exhale and lay back on the cushions.

"Typhoid," she grumbled, grabbing the cat and burrowing a few kisses into the feline's neck. "Your timing is really terrible, you know that?" With that, she flopped backwards on the couch.

Typhoid's response to that was to curl up on Ellie's heaving chest and feign sleep, purring loudly. Ellie bit back a giggle and stroked the cat's thick fur.

"Oh, Ty," Ellie said as the cat opened one uninterested green eye at her, "why can't I find a wild and crazy guy like Brady Garriston in this little backwater town?"

THREE

"No way!" Cal downed his beer and was waving a nearby waiter over to bring a refill.

Brady swallowed a bite of hamburger. After nearly a hundred foreign meals sampled throughout the European continent, the innocuous, unadorned slab of meat tasted funny. It had not occurred to him that he might get sick acclimating himself again to American food after a long absence. "I'm serious," he answered finally.

"No!"

"Yes!" Brady answered Cal with equal insistence.

Cal shook his head, incredulous. He rolled his eyes as he sipped the fresh beer set before him. "No, no. I refuse to believe it." He waved his finger in Brady's face. "You can't tell me that you flew halfway across the freakin' world and didn't see any action. I mean, come on! The women there!"

Brady drowned a French fry in the puddle of ketchup on his plate. "Yes?" For all the bassist's experience and reputation in the music business, he knew the closest Cal Briscoe ever came to a European trip was a weekend at Disney's EPCOT Center. Cal was not one to tour off the continent. What did he know of the women there? Or of the women at EPCOT, even?

Cal now appeared flustered, stammering on several aborted words before finally saying, "They sell condoms in Europe, don't they?" in a low voice.

Brady, trying his best at a straight face, ate the red fry and chewed thoughtfully. "I believe they do, Cal. Not that I checked specifically for them, you know, because I was more concerned with finding my own way around the more popular attractions like the Coliseum and Stonehenge rather than the finer drugstores of Europe."

"Oh." Cal appeared chagrined. "I must be thinking of Africa, where they don't have condoms. All those kids with flies buzzing on their faces, pitiful," he added, then took a big bite of his own hamburger.

Brady, letting Cal's word sink in, set his down on its plate. Had his friend just said that out loud?

"Like I wanna hear about the Catacombs and rows of dead buried popes, anyway. I'm half-Jewish, for crying out loud, like I care," grumbled Cal. "Sounds like a wasted trip to me."

"Actually, I enjoyed the tour of Vatican City. It was a very spiritual experience," Brady replied, keeping his frustrations in check. Cal was slowly getting drunk, it was obvious; by tomorrow it seemed unlikely to Brady that the musician would remember any of their conversation.

"I figured a guy like you would like that place," Cal said.

"How's that?"

Cal snorted. "You stuck in a city full of people

who never get laid either."

"Lay off," Brady grumbled, and pushed aside his refill. The alcohol had done nothing to improve his state of mind, and the way things were going now this inebriated conversation with Cal would not help, nor would it endear Cal to him when it came time to choose musicians for his next project. Whenever he decided to begin a new project, *if* he could begin one. "Isn't it enough that I have to suffer jet lag, I have to listen to you yapping about my sex life?"

Or lack thereof.

Cal continued as if not hearing his friend. "All I'm saying is how can a guy spend nearly two months tooling around places where sex comes free with a tank of gas, and he doesn't get some!"

"Well, mostly I took subways and buses," Brady replied as Cal laughed.

Brady now pushed away his half-eaten sandwich. As his best friend, Cal knew quite a bit about Brady's uninhibited past, and had even been witness or participant in some of the rowdier moments of their youth. Cal knew also, though, that in the last decade and a half that Brady had become more selective and cautious when taking a woman to bed, sometimes waiting months, if he did at all.

He did not wait that long with Claire, though. Despite her straight-laced attitude, Claire had excited him, and he thought that proof enough that opposites did indeed attract.

Yet she dumped him anyway. Brady shook

his head. Showed what he knew. Some things he would just never figure out.

"So anyway, Johnson's gone to LA," Cal was saying, picking up from another topic of conversation that was the focus before he launched into the European sex queries. "Got a job scoring this new daytime soap. Chelsea hired Danny Moore for lead guitar."

Brady shook his head. "Don't know him."

"I'll introduce you. He'd be great to have around when you're ready to go back to work."

"I don't know if I will or not." Brady's voice was mournful and quiet, and he could tell Cal was not listening for the slurping noise made with his own glass. Just as well, Brady decided. He didn't want to risk turning their conversation down an uglier avenue.

"Your burger no good, Brady?" Cal asked.

Brady looked up from his plate. "Huh? Oh, it's fine. I guess I just lost my appetite."

Cal nodded. "Jet lag. Gets you every time. Happens to me when I fly to LA. Can't eat for days. May I?" He gestured to Brady's plate and helped himself to the untouched pickle spear, bobbing his head up and down to a distant piano rhythm.

Then came the words Brady dreaded, through a mouth filled with pickle and hamburger. "Hey, how's that Claire chick you were seeing? She know you're back yet?"

What Brady had eaten of his dinner roiled in his stomach and threatened a return appearance. He took a deep drink from his glass to quay the nausea. "I don't know," he croaked. "We sort of ended things when I left."

"Too bad," Cal mumbled. "She seemed like a class act. If you weren't my best friend I'd give her a call." His face fell. "Right. Like she would go for a *schmo* like me."

Brady took another deep swig of beer. "You're not a *schmo*, Cal, but you're right. I don't think she'd go for you." If she thought *Brady* needed to grow up…

"So she's into *schmo* rock stars then," Cal accused.

"I'm more like a *schmo* ex-rock star." Brady still had no idea what he was going to do for work. As many pens and journals lay around his house, they were useless to him so long as his mental inkwell was dry.

"Having trouble coming up with new material?"

Brady nodded.

"Happens to the best of them. Maybe you should get away," Cal suggested.

"Cal, I just got back from Europe, for crying out loud."

Cal shrugged. "I don't mean go on a vacation. I mean go somewhere else and start over. Maybe you've tapped all you can out of the city. So, why not go to LA? You could find some film work, something to tide you over until your really serious creative juices start flowing again."

"What? Just go to LA and pound off a stream of ridiculous filler movie songs?"

"Worked for Randy Newman, didn't it?"

Brady watched his friend polish off both of

their plates as if he had not eaten in a week. His demeanor gave a whole new dimension to the starving artist persona, and it prompted a genuine smile from Brady, because Cal had money.

Though the thought of selling out to Hollywood made him feel dirty, Cal's idea had some merit. Maybe he did need more than a vacation to regain his creativity. Maybe he had not stayed away from New York long enough.

Plus, Claire had made it clear they were finished, and she implied she was seeing other men. Brady surmised he really had no reason to stay in New York.

"So, you didn't see any action in Europe, huh?" Cal broke into Brady's thoughts.

"I told you already," Brady said, annoyed. "I didn't go there to be the continental bicycle, offering everybody a free ride."

"Figures. You are truly a freak of nature, my friend. When I think of all the stories your peers have told me over the years…hell, when I think of all the things, and people, you and I did together! You used to be just as horny, and willing, as the rest of them. Now, you couldn't get laid even if you had the words 'Fuck Me' tattooed on your forehead," Cal challenged, stifling a belch. "Which I noticed, by the way, is getting more and more visible."

I'm horny now. But it had nothing to do with Cal. Brady signaled a passing waiter for the check. "You're in a mood," he said. "I don't blame Chelsea for running off with the drummer."

"The Little Drummer Boy." Cal snickered.

"Chelsea's not going to get much rum-pa-pum-pum tonight, I'll tell you that. If the stories I hear about *him* are true."

"Why I'm still friends with you I'll never know." Looking toward the opposite end of the bar, near the active piano and cigarette machine, Brady furrowed his brows. "Oh, look at that."

"What?" Cal lowered his glass.

"I think we got trouble."

Brady cocked his head toward a small round table illuminated weakly by a burning votive candle. A slender blonde in a dark green dress with spaghetti straps was arguing heatedly with a thick, olive-skinned man occupying the chair next to her. Clearly he had been uninvited, not to mention drinking more than Brady and Cal put together, and he was unsuccessfully trying to paw the woman's shoulders. Brady could clearly see the agitation on the young woman's face, despite the dim lighting. She was pale and beautiful, and looked remarkably like Claire in the face.

Brady squeezed his eyes shut. Maybe Cal was right to suggest that he leave the city, but would that do any good? He would continue to see Claire everywhere he would go, he knew.

Cal stood and tapped Brady's shoulder. "We should go over there," he said, suddenly sober and serious.

"And do what? We're not cops," Brady said. "Let the manager handle it."

"No," Cal insisted. "I don't like bullies, particularly bullies fond of groping women without permission. This girl could be Melissa, for Pete's sake."

Brady's swallowed back the bile rising in his throat. Yes, he would want somebody to come to Melissa's rescue if ever she were in this situation. Without another word, he followed Cal to the blonde's table.

"This guy bothering you, miss?" Cal asked.

The woman looked up from her unwanted, intoxicated suitor with a frown. "Very much," she replied pointedly, swatting away the man's eager hands. The drunkard, however, was only encouraged by her resistance and chuckled loudly.

Presently two waiters approached, prepared to quash the brewing fracas. Neither Brady nor Cal paid them heed. "Okay, bucko, you heard the lady. Up we go." Cal stepped behind the man's chair and jerked the man upward with a clamp to the shoulders.

"H-Hey!" he slurred as Brady winced at the sudden output of gin fumes. "I was talking to my girlfriend here."

"I'm not your girlfriend," the woman said coldly. "I've never seen you before in my life. I don't even know your name."

"Oh, sorry about that." The man wriggled free and wobbled over the woman's head, extending his hand toward her chest. "G-G-George."

The woman looked up at the man in disbelief. "You trying to shake my breasts, buddy?"

Brady blushed slightly at this.

"That's it, enough," Cal said, grabbing the guy again and beckoning the waiters with a crook of the neck. The larger of the two moved in to grab the man's other arm. "Hey, friend, let's call it a night, huh?" he said to Brady. "I'm going to put this asshole G-G-George in a cab and see that he gets home, wherever that is."

"What?" Brady frowned. "You sure you want to do that? You don't know this guy. He could be dangerous."

Cal and the waiter, however, were already dragging the drunk like a heavy sack out the door. "I'll be fine. I was in the mood for some excitement tonight, anyway, and your boring stories aren't doing it for me," he called. "I'll call you tomorrow."

"Wha?" George looked from Cal to the waiter to Brady and back. "No, nooo. I wanna stay and shake hands with this lady." And he disappeared with his party through the paneled double doors.

"Okay, I guess I'll cover dinner," Brady replied softly. He was probably going to, anyway. One of the reasons Cal had so much money was because he seldom picked up a check.

He turned back to the woman, who sulked in her chair, arms folded and ready to snap at the first person who tried to speak to her. Brady decided to risk it nonetheless.

"Everything all right?" he asked her. Up close, the resemblance to Claire was not as prominent; this woman wore her hair longer, and her face appeared stronger with more defined cheekbones. Perhaps, however, that was because she was clenching her teeth, annoyed.

The woman did not look up at him. "I'll be fine, thank you."

"Uh, I notice that guy spilled your drink... I could have them freshen it up for you."

Her head craned upward, flashing eyes of ice. "How many more men being dragged away from here is it going to take for me just to enjoy a lousy drink by myself?" she snapped.

Brady rocked back on his heels, hands in his pockets, feeling suddenly like a fool. "Right," he finally whispered, wanting to crawl under the floorboards. "Sorry to have bothered you," he added politely before inching back to his table. She obviously had not recognized him, a rarity in the city, or anywhere else.

He flipped his American Express card on the table as the waiter materialized to clear away the plates. "Get you another beer, Mr. Garriston?" he asked.

Brady shook his head and asked for a Dewars neat to add to the bill, though he knew he really did not need one. He was still not ready to go home, however; there was nothing there for him.

"Sure thing, sir. By the way, tell your friend thanks for getting rid of that asshole."

"I'll do that. What happened to your piano player?"

The waiter craned his neck toward the now silent instrument. "Oh, his shift must be over. He usually quits early on Fridays so he can party with everybody else."

Brady looked around the small restaurant; there was still a healthy crowd gathered around tables and the bar, smoking and drinking and chattering. Nobody appeared to notice that the music had stopped, so perhaps nobody would mind him. It had been a while since he played.

"May I?" Brady gestured to the piano.

The waiter eyed him with amusement. "Have at it. Too bad the boss isn't here tonight. He's a big fan."

"Be that as it may, I think I'll stick with the standards tonight, thanks." Brady sauntered over to the piano. Settling himself on the bench and testing a few keys, he immediately launched into "The Man Who Got Away" from *A Star is Born*, pleased to see he had not lost his touch.

The crowd remained focused in their own conversations, but a few female heads turned from the bar to enjoy the music and admire the musician, whispering to each other with awe. Brady cast a sideways glance and could easily read one pair of lips. *You know who that is, don't you?*

Seconds later the waiter approached with Brady's drink, setting it on the piano and slipping a ten spot in the empty brandy glass already there. "That's from the brunette in the blue slacks and white jacket."

Brady leaned past the waiter's slim body to see the lovely lady tipper raise her wineglass in greeting. Brady nodded acknowledgement and smiled.

It felt good to be at the piano again, even if he was not playing his own material. Just the touch of the keys beneath his fingers sparked a satisfaction in him that had been missing while he was away. He wanted to attribute his lack of songwriting prowess abroad to the lack of access to a piano, but that would have been a feeble argument. He could make things happen wherever he was; Europe had pianos, too, so there were no excuses. At the piano, playing music, was where he was supposed to be.

All he needed to do now was harness that desire into new material. He needed inspiration, however. Shapely, sexy inspiration.

He played for the better part of a half-hour without stopping to rest, segueing from Gershwin to Porter, Bacharach to the Beatles, fielding the occasional request shouted from a table provided he knew the song. Smatterings of applause followed the end of each song, and as the night wore on and the gentle music filled his ears, Brady began to feel better. The awkward phone call with Claire was nearly forgotten.

He finished up "Candle in the Wind," a request from the waiter, with his eyes closed, trying to recall the sheet music in his mind. He sensed another person closing in on him and he opened his eyes just in time to see a delicate hand dip inside the brandy glass to release a dollar bill.

"Well, hello there," he said to the woman in the green dress. "Any requests?"

A thick clump of hair fell in front of the woman's eyes, and she brushed it back with the free hand; the other one clasped her sweating highball glass. "I-I'm sorry about before," she said with a weak smile. "It's just that I'm visiting the city for the first time on an extended vacation, and I guess I'm a bit intimidated by everything and everybody here."

"Not a problem." Brady tinkered with the black keys. "Where you from?"

"You wouldn't know the place," she said. "A really tiny town in Virginia. One stoplight, blink and you'll miss it."

Brady nodded. He thought he had detected a southern twang in her voice. "Well, I'd play 'Carry Me Home to Old Virginia' for you, but I'm afraid I don't know it."

"Don't worry, neither do I," the woman assured him. She put out her free hand. "I'm Sue Carmichael."

"Pleased to meet you, Sue," he began, then paused. Would it be wise to reveal himself to her, since she still did not appear to recognize him? He did not know why he felt so self-conscious about it all of a sudden. Surely there existed people in the world who had not heard of Brady Garriston, just as there were people who had not heard of The Beatles or Elvis, rare as those people were. Still, Brady decided he was enjoying the anonymity of this evening, and he would probably never see this woman again.

"I'm Gary," he said finally. "Gary Stone." He gladly accepted her hand, still tapping piano keys with the other one.

"You play the piano well, Gary," Sue said.

"It is one thing I haven't managed to mess up in my life, yes," he agreed. "What would you like to hear? What's your favorite song?"

A playful smile curled her lips. "'Rhiannon' by Fleetwood Mac."

"Okay, it goes like this, right?" he asked,

pounding out the opening notes to "Linus and Lucy."

Sue erupted with laughter. "No!" she chided. Whooping encouragement wafted over from a distant table.

Brady lifted his fingers from the keyboard, the final notes echoing into silence. "I'm sorry, then," he said, trying to conceal his smile. "I guess I don't know that one."

"Then play some more Elton John. I love him," she suggested, shocking Brady with a rather brazen move by taking a seat on the edge of the bench. He obliged her by inching to the right. She smelled of vanilla, and the pale skin visible in the deep neck of her dress looked soft to the touch. A flicker of want teased his senses and he pictured Sue Carmichael of One Stoplight, Virginia topless, his tongue swirling around a hardened nipple.

Man, I need to get laid. He was going to explode right here at this piano if he didn't control himself.

He took a deep breath. "Elton, huh. You and my ex-wife and daughter," he said, slowly launching into "Tiny Dancer." He focused on the keyboard, channeling his energy into the music, morphing song after song together into one long melody. It helped little when Sue leaned closer to watch him play, so he kept his mind busy trading quips and laughs over the songs. He even tried to get her to sing along with him to the music, only to discover that their singing voices were not compatible.

Her body…now *that* looked compatible. Sue

Carmichael was definitely an attractive woman, one who could easily mend a broken heart with the simplest of smiles. Right now, her round hip brushing against his tightened thigh was enough to set his cock stirring once again.

Awkwardly he shifted in place to ease the ache. The woman had said the city intimidated her; the last thing she needed to see was whom she perceived to be a restaurant piano player with a massive erection tenting his slacks.

Man, he gasped inwardly. Even in his rambunctious youth, he never recalled being this aroused so often.

Quite unconsciously, Sue checked her watch and blanched. Immediately she broke contact and leaped from the bench. "Oh, man," she exclaimed. "It's after midnight! I didn't expect to be out this late."

"Midnight's not late in New York." Brady finished his rendition of "A Fine Romance" with a flourish. "You must still be on tiny, one-stoplight Virginia town time."

"I guess so, but still, I'm beat." Sue plucked a credit card from her pocketbook and waved a waiter over to the piano with it. Brady lowered her hand with his.

"Don't worry about it," he winked. "I got your tab."

"Oh, Gary, you don't have to."

"I want to."

Sue blushed deep red, slipping the card into a slit in her wallet. "Thanks. You're so sweet. I owe you one. If you're ever in my neck of the woods…"

"I'm holding you to that." Brady tapped the middle C, his eyes staring straight ahead. "Anyway, you don't owe me a thing. You don't realize what you did for me tonight. I didn't come here in the best of moods." He turned to her. "But now I'm feeling much better. In fact, I probably owe you more than the drinks."

Sue leaned even closer. Brady felt his entire body stiffen this time. He willed her to a quick exit. Two more seconds and he would be playing the next song with no hands.

"Thank you again," she whispered. "This is definitely the highlight of my trip so far." And she kissed his cheek and rose.

Brady watched Sue glide gracefully to the front doors, noting many male eyes studying her as she pushed through the exit without so much as a backward glance. He sighed. She was very attractive indeed. He wondered if, given a bit more time, he could have had her in a cab and in his bed within the hour.

He shook his head. The old Brady was resurfacing. Damn Cal and his badgering.

Had the old Brady ever really gone away, though? Fleeing to Europe after being dumped was the sort of impetuous thing he would have done at twenty. At fifty, it seemed…

Immature.

Well, he thought, *maybe I* like *being immature.* He should be thanking Cal, he supposed.

Then he smiled. Sue had not recognized him at all. He liked that, too. He liked being Gary

Stone, even if just for the night. Gary Stone seemed to be happier and more adjusted than Brady Garriston, and given the chance he could probably be as successful a musician, if not more so.

His fingers stilled on the keys. Gary Stone did not necessarily have to go away tonight, did he?

"Hey, Piano Man!" bellowed a burly man at the bar, waking Brady from his reverie. "You know 'New York State of Mind'?"

"This is your lucky night, my friend." Brady flexed his aching fingers and once again became the house musician, humming along to the Billy Joel tune, thinking about Sue and Claire and Gary Stone. The more he thought, the more he realized Cal's idea of starting over elsewhere made sense. Perhaps he could find another place to be...as another person.

He could use Gary Stone to bring forth his creativity again, and he could write songs. Perhaps, too, he could find a proper balance between his immature self and the grown man Claire wanted in her life and become that person.

Perhaps he would try to get in touch with Claire later, and she would see this new, improved, self and talk to him again. Go out with him again, just for the hell of it.

Perhaps he would learn to play "Rhiannon," too.

FOUR

He returned to his apartment around three, with his trousers pockets stuffed with currency. He had tried to leave the money in the brandy glass for the restaurant's regular entertainment, but the wait staff had insisted he take the money. The patrons had left it for him, and they had refused to take it themselves when Brady offered them the money.

"You earned it," one waiter had told him. "We take only what we earn." Brady recalled how the others chuckled when their spokesman suggested he not spend it all in one place.

Brady had no need for the crumpled bills. Standing in front of his guarded building, he spied a homeless man curled in an Army blanket at the left corner. Wordlessly, he approached and handed the poor being the night's gain.

The transient offered up a toothless smile as he took the bills with a dirty hand. Brady countered the bar patrons' tips with a twenty from his own wallet before retreating upstairs.

"Don't spend it all in one place," he said with a sad smile before entering his building. He strode past the reception desk and nodded to Jared, the night clerk.

A slim man of about twenty-two with coal

black hair and eyes and sharp facial features, Jared looked up from the comic novel he was reading and smiled. Per the relaxed dress code of the night watch, the young man had eschewed the heavier formal topcoat of the day clerks for a simple white shirt and black jeans. "Mr. G, welcome back. How was Europe?"

Brady slid past the first elevator door that opened and returned Jared's slight wave. "Still there, left it as I found it," he said, and the door slid closed before Jared could say anything more.

When he reached his apartment he was still not tired, and had no desire to wind down into sleep. Thoughts of transforming into Gary Stone occupied his mind, and he wanted to formulate a plan while the idea and the intent was still fresh. After shedding his clothes for a more comfortable pair of sweat shorts and T-shirt, he grabbed the last soda in his scantily stocked refrigerator, padded to his bedroom, and fired up his Internet connection. Within seconds he had a political map of the country in one browser window and a search engine gathering a listing of real estate Web sites on another.

He leaned back in his office chair, propping a bare foot on the edge of the desk. *Where to go?* He wanted to remain close to home, so Los Angeles was not an option for him. Though his daughter had joyfully embraced her independence, he still wanted to be close enough to fly home within a few hours if he needed to do so. Plus, if Claire ever called while he was away...

Right. Don't hold your breath. Get over it.

He studied the eastern seaboard. Cal had mentioned once before a recording studio in the Virginia Beach area where a number of famous names had recorded. The shore town was secluded enough to permit anonymity, and was a short plane ride back to the city. He could find a nice spot to plant a beach chair and gaze out toward the Chesapeake Bay, and dine on jimmy crabs and cold beer every day if he wanted. Write songs, be the north's answer to Jimmy Buffett, convert a few music lovers to his sound, and maybe renew the interest of his regular fans in the process, people who might otherwise have written him off as finished.

It was definitely a possibility. Brady clicked the mouse on the state to enlarge the graphic. Finding a condominium to rent in the area should not prove difficult.

Virginia. Wasn't that where his new friend Sue said she came from? He never did catch the name of that one stoplight town, which could have been anywhere in the diverse state—close to the political action in Washington, D.C., tucked high in the Appalachian Mountains, or close to the sun-kissed shores of the Tidewater area he was currently perusing.

He rolled the mouse's pointer over a name in tiny print that caught his eye. *Dareville.* According to the map, it was not far from the beach, and judging by the size of the word on the map it could hardly qualify as the county seat. An interesting name for a town, it was, sparking thoughts of spontaneity and adventure.

It seemed like the kind of place where he could disappear, where Gary Stone would live. He did not need to see the place to know it was exactly what he wanted.

He flipped to the search engine window and erased the data given him, then began a new search for Dareville real estate. The requests did not yield many results, but at this moment he wasn't picky. Neither, he knew, was Gary Stone.

Brady leaned back and closed his eyes. Dareville. Intriguing name for a small town, yes. Images of dogwood trees lining one-lane roads filtered into his mind. Acres of peanut plants dotting the landscape, the sun bearing down on white-shuttered Colonial homes with large porches. People drinking iced tea, moving much slower than in the city.

He chuckled. Yes, it was nice to idealize things, and he hoped his expectations of little Dareville wouldn't be dashed by reality.

A quick check of the real estate Web site, thankfully, confirmed his suspicions of the town. There were some nice old houses available for sale and rent, and glowing commentary of Dareville's small town charm and friendly residents, family-owned businesses, and proximity to many Virginia points of interest. He jotted down a few phone numbers with a reminder to make some calls in the morning.

"Okay, then," he muttered, and checked his e-mail. His address was private, and he had chosen a user name one would hardly associate with him, so there was never the bother of wading through a long list of fan messages. Junk e-mail, however, he could not avoid, and he clicked his mouse with abandon, hoping not to catch some kind of computer virus.

He was not fast enough, however, to avoid missing a blatant advertisement for a pornographic Web site, arriving in an e-mail message that prompted a pop-up browser window to fill his screen with images of surgically-enhanced female models licking each other's shaved privates. A more prudish Web surfer might have paled at the explicit sight, but Brady only scoffed, closed the browser, and proceeded to clear the cache on his hard drive.

"Sorry, guys," he sang. "Never had to pay for it before, not going to start." Besides, he found pornography boring and took no pleasure in such magazines or watching films, not even as a precursor to foreplay. Why sit on the sidelines and watch while others had all the fun?

He sighed. Thoughts of Claire resurfaced, only this time they mingled with images of lovely Sue from the restaurant. What were they doing right now? What pleasures might they have found in the city since he saw them last? Sure, Sue had said she was going back to her hotel, but he could not be certain of that. The city had a knack for making people, especially tourists, do things they otherwise might not consider. Perhaps she might catch the eye of a handsome valet at her hotel, going off-duty and looking for some excitement.

What happens in New York might not always

stay in New York, but to be sure, nobody is going to give you grief about it.

He closed his eyes; both women were completely in focus now behind his eyelids, pliant to his imagination. Suddenly they were naked, pouting and preening at him, then at each other. In his mind he willed them to kiss, then to fondle each other's breasts, then to lie back against the swirling dream backdrop in which they floated and intertwined their bodies around each other in passionate embrace, kissing and caressing each other.

You hypocrite. For all his disdain of porn, what was he doing now but fantasizing about two women, creating a stag loop in his head? He felt the twitch in his groin as fantasy Claire's open mouth slid down fantasy Sue's throat to capture one of Sue's erect nipples, sucking and nibbling at her flesh while her hands aggressively kneaded the other woman's buttocks.

Brady smiled, and instinctively felt for the growing bulge in his shorts. The image in his mind then skipped forward, like a satellite feed glitch, because now Claire had shifted position. She lay stretched opposite Sue now in sixty-nine mode, her face hovering over Sue's slick pussy while she curiously fingered the smooth, pink folds. With a desirous smile, her tongue shot downward and stroked the throbbing clit, then lapped at the juices dripping between the other woman's thighs.

"Nice," he murmured aloud, stroking his hardened cock through his shorts. He could only imagine Sue was reciprocating the favor in this fantasy, as he only concentrated on Claire. For a few more seconds, at least.

The sharp buzz of his doorbell sounded throughout the apartment, jarring him awake. He nearly fell from his chair.

"Shit!" He reached across his desk and depressed a button on a portable device that served as an intercom and automated door lock. One of the perks of living in one the higher end apartments of the building; he did not have to walk all the way to the front door to see who was there. "Who is it?" he demanded. Who possibly could be bothering him in the wee hours?

Jared's deep voice crackled through the pinholes. "I tried to tell you before the elevator closed that the cleaners delivered your suits while you were gone," he said. "I got 'em right here for you."

Brady frowned. Suits? He had suits that needed to be cleaned? Then he realized Melissa must have arranged for that, if only to have an excuse to catch sight of Jared, whom Brady knew the girl found attractive.

This could not, however, wait until morning? Of course, it *was* morning, technically, and maybe Jared was looking for something to do beside sit at the desk. It was common knowledge around the building that Brady kept odd hours and likely would not be bothered so late.

Brady sighed. "Okay, come on in," he called, and pressed another button that unlocked his front door. Perks.

Jared loped into his bedroom. His fingers were looped around several hangers holding suits that draped down his back, all covered in clear plastic. "Where to, chief?" he asked with a grin.

Brady nodded toward his open closet door. "Anywhere in there is fine," he told the young man, and leaned back to close his eyes again. Blood pounded in his head and coursed a sensuous heat through his body that he needed to ease immediately. He was going to have to take another shower when Jared left, he knew, instinctively flexing his right hand. How pathetic was that?

He also knew, unfortunately, that Jared was rather talkative and would probably not be so eager to head back to the front desk.

No sense in fighting the inevitable, he decided. Maybe if he initiated conversation, he could control it completely, make it short, and have Jared out of his hair so he could jack off in peace.

"You still in school?" He heard the clacking of metal against metal as Jared arranged the hangers.

"Yeah," came the reply. "Last semester, all internship. It's going to be a breeze."

"And you're still doing journalism, right?"

"Uh-huh. I'll be starting at the *Post* next we—"

Brady's eyes shot open as the young man's voice faded, and he raised an eyebrow. Jared was staring at him, mouth agape in disbelief. His sudden silence baffled Brady momentarily—few things could render the young man speechless, he knew, and when he followed Jared's eyes to the source of his shock he finally understood.

Jared had his eyes on Brady's erection, which was tenting the thin fabric of his shorts, seeking release.

Brady felt flushed, and debated whether or not to reach down and shift his hard-on to a more presentable, less visible, position, if one existed. To have Jared staring at him was awkward, yet at the same time he couldn't help but be turned on, particularly since the young man's expression seemed to hold a touch of awe. Perhaps Jared was envious that he was not similarly blessed in this department.

Or maybe...was that awe in the young man's eyes, or interest?

Brady smiled. If his instincts were correct, Melissa was going to be *so* disappointed.

"Jared," he began, his voice huskier than intended.

Jared swallowed and finally met Brady's eyes. "I-I'm sorry," he said quietly. "I didn't mean to stare. I mean—"

"I don't mind, Jared. People have been staring at me for thirty years." Brady shifted in his seat and crossed one leg over the other to conceal his erection. The action caused Jared's expression immediately to darken into disappointment. So he *was* interested, interested in more than just looking.

Brady lifted the leg just as quickly, then spread his knees farther apart so that his erection was even more prominent, close to slipping through one leg of his shorts. A shift in the right direction would have the tip peeking out at the young man like a curious, burrowed mammal.

He tried it. Peek-a-boo. The audible catch in Jared's throat was unmistakable.

Brady smiled. He could not help but be flattered by Jared's response. "Like what you see?"

"Oh, yeah." Jared's smile seemed embarrassed, and Brady bit back a laugh. He had his suspicions of some of the other clerks in the building, but Jared surprised him. He wondered if Jared really was gay, or at the most straddled the fence. It did not bother Brady one way or the other, though.

He was not one to judge. Brady himself had experimented sexually with other men in his randy youth, always while strung out on something illegal, which rendered him willing to take on anybody interested. Thankfully, the few same-sex partners he had remained mum in order to preserve their own reputations and audiences. Or maybe, since it had been so long ago and the participants were so drunk or stoned, they just could not remember anything.

Still, Brady never considered himself gay, or bisexual. He could not call himself bi-curious, either, since his curiosity had long ago been satisfied.

Right now, watching Jared watch his cock straining against his thigh, he could only think of one word to describe himself: *horny*. He had gone without physical contact with another person for two months, and that was fifty-nine days too long.

Scratch that. He was horny and welcoming of any opportunity at this point, caution be damned. A quickie with the night clerk would be preferable to another lonely session of treating himself like a slot machine. Jared was a warm body, and Brady ached for another person's touch.

If only Jared was Claire, though. Or Sue, or any woman.

He thought a moment. Maybe Claire dumped him because she suspected Brady might eventually cheat on her, perceptive as she was about his spontaneity. But since they were no longer a couple, he was not cheating now. If she had not dumped him, not turned down his offer for a meeting tonight, she would not have to have worried about his attentions being directed elsewhere. He would have been hers for the night.

He held Jared's smoldering gaze. His cock throbbed against his thigh. So what if Jared was a guy? He needed this now. Gary Stone could wait a few hours to surface. *Claire, you had your chance*.

He had to be sure Jared was willing to go beyond this voyeurism, though. He was not going to force himself on anybody. At the very least, the young man had not fled the apartment in shock or disgust upon seeing him like this.

He reached behind his neck and pulled off his T-shirt. His nipples were tight, and he pinched one, hoping to draw away from the more obvious ache below. Jared's smile widened; the young man was clearly warming to the unspoken suggestion between them.

"You got a few minutes to spare, don't you?" he asked Jared, already knowing the answer. Night clerks worked in pairs; there was somebody else downstairs, probably reading Jared's comic book right now, being bored. Let that guy handle any unlikely emergencies.

Brady lifted his ass slightly from the chair and slid off his shorts, which he kicked to one side. A drop of precum bubbled at the tip of his erection, and he massaged it over his shaft, noting the hungry look on Jared's face, the way his chest heaved and his hands tensed at his sides. The young man needed no further prodding—Jared looked ready to dive headfirst into his crotch—but Brady beckoned him closer with a crook of the neck anyway to confirm his approval.

Three broad steps forward brought Jared to his knees before Brady, and without further pretense he cuffed one hand around Brady's cock and took it deep into his mouth, working the shaft up and down with moderate speed. A low groan escaped Brady's lips upon contact. It felt so good to have somebody fuck him like this again. Male, female, it was all good, so long as the end result was an incredible orgasm. He closed his eyes...

...to see Claire kneeling in Jared's place. Whatever she had done with the now absent fantasy Sue was over, leaving her free to service him. He watched as Claire tackled his erection with gusto, swirling her tongue around the aching tip and sliding her pursed lips up and down one side of his shaft before swallowing him whole again, driving him to the edge of ecstasy.

He ran his fingers through her short hair, holding her to him. "Damn, but you're good at this," he rumbled. Claire's response was to squeeze one of his thighs, then walk her fingers inward to stroke the underside of his scrotum.

"Do you want me to come in your mouth? I'm about there." He could feel the buildup clear to his toes, and was disappointed somewhat when the tightened, wet hold on his cock released.

The gruff, negative answer surprised him, and Brady's eyes bolted open. Claire was gone, and he saw that he had a grip on Jared's dark locks. The young man was staring up at him, idly stroking the base of his shaft.

He shook his head, he should have known. The real Claire had refused to do this to him that night. The mere suggestion that she participate in pleasuring a woman for his benefit would probably have sent her through the roof.

He smoothed down Jared's hair and smiled. "What do you want, then?"

There was a tremor in Jared's voice. "I want you to fuck my ass."

Brady almost had to laugh at the way Jared had said it, like the young man was asking for permission to be fucked, or expecting rejection. Brady instead let the back of his hand slide down Jared's cheek, then curl around the young man's neck.

"Come here," he whispered, and Jared rose slightly to lean forward, allowing Brady to draw him into a gentle kiss. Jared's lips were chapped and tasted salty, his skin was rough against his own with the beginnings of a beard.

Brady ran his tongue along Jared's lower lip, nipping it slightly between his teeth. "You are a very good-looking man," he said. He leaned back to allow Jared to brush a hand over his chest. "I'm surprised somebody hasn't already snatched you up."

Jared dipped low to run his tongue over one of Brady's nipples. "I'm not really looking for commitment right now," he said. "I just want to have fun."

Brady nodded. That was what he had wanted at Jared's age. How long ago had that been? Now there was this desire to start over again, grow up, and it confused him.

Right now, though, he just wanted to come. He did not care how he got there.

He could feel the heat of Jared's blush in their awkward embrace, and was not surprised to hear the quiver in the young man's voice.

"You don't have to do this, Mr. G," he said. "I know you're not really gay—"

He broke away and eased to stand. "You don't have to call me Mr. G. anymore, either, and I do what I want," he said. "Let me duck into the bathroom real quick," he told Jared, then advised the young man to get undressed.

He had not expected Jared to comply so quickly, however. He emerged from his bathroom, sheathed and erect and carrying a small container of petroleum jelly, to find Jared's lean, naked body reclining sideways on the bed, head propped on his elbow. Brady smiled. Jared had an incredible body, hairless and taut like an Olympic swimmer's, one that should have been modeling for underwear ads instead of being hunched over a comic book or the city desk of a metropolitan newspaper. He was certainly enticing enough to tempt any straight man to switch teams.

Yet Brady had no desire to reciprocate the blowjob or have Jared penetrate either of his orifices with his equally impressive cock. What he needed, wanted, was his own release. Jared, watching him with obvious lust, clearly wanted only one thing as well, and that suited Brady fine. It had been a while since he had performed anal sex, though it was something he enjoyed—on the giving end, of course.

Without being prompted, the young man turned to support himself on all fours. Brady positioned himself behind Jared and ran his free hand over the young man's bent bottom before parting the cheeks to reveal the puckered target. He teased Jared with a slight touch, then settled his cock between Jared's ass cheeks and rubbed it back and forth. He felt Jared twitch with delight.

"You have such a nice, tight ass," he said. Jared did not reply, but Brady could sense he was blushing.

Brady dipped a finger into the tiny vat he held and scraped a dollop of the opaque yellow goo. He leaned over Jared's curved back, running his free hand up one side and down Jared's right arm. Jared trembled slightly from the touch, then gasped as the jelly-coated finger thrust between his buttocks and deep into his anus.

"How do you like it?" Brady buzzed into his ear. "How do you want me to fuck you?"

"Hard and fast," came a quivering reply.

And Brady straightened, then complied. He positioned the tip of his shaft against Jared's anus and pushed forward with a low growl. He could hear Jared cry slightly at the contact, then moan his approval, and for a fleeting moment Brady wondered how much cock the young man had taken in during past dalliances.

Soon, though, Brady's eyes closed and he no longer saw Jared. This time it was One Stoplight Sue's turn. Her rounded ass was pressed against him, being pounded as she looked back at him through her drooping bangs, licking her lips and enjoying every minute of it.

"You feel so good. God, I'm glad you asked me to do this," he groaned. She was so beautiful, and so tight around his cock it was nearly impossible to move even with all the lubricant. "You like that, babe?"

Her breasts were pendulous, swaying with every deep, grinding stroke. "Fuck, yes," he heard her moan. "Don't stop."

He picked up speed. Mattress coils cried underneath them. The headboard rattled. Sue lifted herself to brace an arm against one bedpost while the other hand reached underneath to stroke her clit. Soon the friction caused by the tightness of her anus was too much for him, and he exploded into orgasm. Her own cry of release was simultaneous and rivaled his in pitch.

Spent, he pulled out and collapsed forward

next to her, the condom he wore slick yet intact. He pulled her close to spoon her and kissed one bare shoulder.

"You don't know how much I needed that," he whispered.

"Glad to be of service, Mr. G."

Brady's eyes shot open as Sue's voice deepened. He was holding Jared now; his hand was grazing the young man's bare chest when it happened upon something wet and warm. He tilted his view forward and realized Jared must have been masturbating while Brady was fucking his ass. The evidence was everywhere.

Brady chuckled and let his hand roam upward to caress Jared's waist and raised hip. He was losing his mind. Dreaming of Claire and Sue, seducing a male night clerk to satisfy his own carnal needs. Regardless of whether or not he wrote another song, he definitely needed to get away, again.

The city does make you do strange things.

"You don't have to—"

"Call you Mr. G. anymore, I know. Sorry, force of habit." Jared turned in Brady's loose grasp so that they faced each other. "It's weird this happened. I've sort of had a thing for you, you know, and I've wondered what it would be like to have you fuck me."

"Really?" Brady arched an eyebrow. "You're into old men?"

"I'm into good-looking men. You're not old."

Brady rewarded his answer with another kiss, this one more intense. Jared's face became willingly pliant as Brady's tongue plundered his mouth; his hands smoothed down Jared's backside and pressed him even closer, so close that he had to lean forward to maintain balance as Jared returned his caresses.

Just as quickly, though, he broke away and eased back on his side. Jared was tempting, and Brady was vulnerable and horny enough for another round. But he did not want to give the young man any ideas. Jared seemed to sense that.

"This isn't going to happen again, is it?" Jared asked.

Brady shrugged. "I never say never." That had been his motto in his youth, and he could only imagine what Cal would have made of his sudden sexual backslide. He probably would have cheered him on, but not before wondering why he just hadn't picked up some babe instead of the night clerk.

"But I am leaving New York again very soon," he added. "Don't know when I'll be back, so—"

Jared smiled. "It's all right, Mr., er, *Brady*." He laughed, and Brady echoed. His name sounded foreign coming from Jared's lips. "It was fun. No regrets."

"None here, either."

Jared eased shyly away, and Brady watched him reach over the side of the bed for a puddle of discarded clothes. Jared's back muscles rippled with every movement; his legs looked like they had been carved from the imagination of a Renaissance sculptor. Melissa was going to be more than disappointed.

Of course, Melissa was never going to find out about this, either.

Brady watched the young man quietly dress. "You want to clean up first?" he asked. "You can use the shower."

He was answered with a vigorous shake of the head. "I'll be fine." Jared's smile was lopsided, the glow of being freshly fucked bright in his eyes. Brady could only wonder what the other night clerk would think of Jared's long absence from delivering suits to the penthouse at three in the morning. "You need anything else?" he asked jokingly.

Brady rolled onto his back, removed the condom from his softening cock, and set it gingerly on the nightstand to his right. "No," he said, "What I need done now, I need to do myself."

Yes, he had to get on the phone with somebody in Dareville, Virginia, as soon as possible, and get out of New York.

I need to do it for *myself. And for my career, and my sanity.*

FIVE

Cousin Claire could keep her fancy four-star restaurants with art deco trimming and plush, burgundy carpets, Ellie decided with a smile as the automatic double doors slid open to grant her admission to Jake's Organic Market. Nothing beat that first step inside Jake's store, especially the immediate aroma of tart, fresh Granny Smiths waiting in a pyramid for her in one display to her left.

She picked the top handheld basket from a stack by the doors and made a beeline for the fruit stand, selecting a few choice apples and a bunch of bananas for future sack lunches. She was about to bypass the rest of the selection when Jake Marbury—slim with silver hair, yet looking much younger and fitter than his sixty years in jeans and a Washington Redskins shirt—wheeled over a cart filled with plastic pint cartons of strawberries.

"Just arrived from Pungo," he announced with pride as Ellie eyed one container in which the berries were bright red and the size of a newborn's fist. She quickly added the container to her basket.

"You sold me, Jake. Of course, I don't know how I'll forgive you for it, since I'll probably *have* to buy some pound cake and whipped cream to go with them." Ellie laughed, and Jake responded in kind.

"Now, Ellie," he said as he positioned the remaining stock on its display, "they're even better by themselves. And better for you."

"If you're willing to carry them in your store, I'll believe it." With a dainty wave, Ellie left the storeowner to tend to his wares and headed for the vegetables. All throughout the school day she had been craving stir-fry for dinner, and she knew she could get out of the market with the ingredients for significantly less than she would if she ordered from the nearest Chinese take-out place. Besides, she much preferred to cook, for at least she would know exactly what was going on her plate and in her body.

Browsing among the bean sprouts and celery, Ellie recognized fellow teacher Lauren McKenna, still dressed from work in pleated beige slacks and white blouse, looking very demure next to Ellie's wild, floral skirt and pink peasant shirt.

Ellie sidled close so that her arm crossed her colleague's line of vision as she reached for a bag of carrots. Lauren woke from whatever deep thought had a hold of her and smiled back.

"Vegging out tonight?" Ellie teased.

Lauren picked at a zucchini. "Low-carb, my friend. That's the way to go this month. Which means no carrots for me, or any other starchy vegetables. The sugar goes straight to your thighs."

Ellie bit back a comment. Clearly the sugar had gone straight to her friend's brain, for Lauren was a toothpick.

"Well, I need the energy," Ellie said, eyeing the broccoli. "I got a stack of spelling and math and penmanship tests knee-deep to grade, and I have to plan for next week."

"Save it, Shaw, I know that dance." Lauren sighed. "At least you don't have to suffer through a building committee meeting tonight as well."

"Right." The building committee for Dareville Primary Academy, formed last year in the wake of a poor state inspection, had been constantly arguing over fundraising ideas for improving the site.

"We just got the estimate on repairs. Yow!" Lauren rolled her eyes. "The contractor told us it would be cheaper to just raze the school and build a new one."

"Well, that would be doable if there were a place to put the children while a new school was being built," Ellie mused, but deep down she knew her words were meaningless. While the private school had only three hundred students from Dareville and surrounding areas, there wasn't an alternative site nearby large enough to house them should there be a need to temporarily vacate the school. Gradual repairs on the current building had to be done.

"The only alternative would be to cut salaries, or entire jobs, and pool that money into the building fund," Lauren said with a shrug, "which we can't afford to do, either."

Ellie shuddered at the thought. The idea of having to compete for a teaching position in Norfolk or Virginia Beach unnerved her, as such jobs were difficult to come by in the present employment market. Having only five years of experience, none in the public sector, hurt her chances as well. Seniority was king among the public schools, in any city.

"Would that help, to get rid of jobs?" Ellie asked, feeling suddenly queasy.

Lauren shook her head, and Ellie relaxed. "Not really. For what the teachers make at DPA, the difference wouldn't be enough to buy new doorknobs." The two women laughed lightly. "Besides," Lauren continued, "we really can't afford to let go of anybody right now."

Ellie understood completely. One reason parents placed their children at DPA, aside from the high standards of education for which the school stood, was the fact that classroom body counts were small, unlike public schools that housed as many as forty to fifty children per teacher. DPA's smaller numbers allowed for teachers to devote more individualized attention where it was needed. Ellie imagined if teachers were let go and classrooms swelled, some parents might be loath to letting their children continue being schooled at DPA.

"That leaves only one other option," Lauren sighed.

"Don't say it." Ellie could read her mind, and she knew as well as anybody on Lauren's committee that no parent would be enthused with the prospect of an astronomical raise in tuition in the middle of the year.

"Everybody wants a better school, but nobody

wants to pay for it. Typical." Lauren made a face and reached for the plastic bag dispenser. "Well, I hope everybody in this town likes Rice Krispies treats, because we are going to be having *a lot* of bake sales."

Lauren followed Ellie's tentative gait toward the rice and pasta aisle. Ellie selected a package of cellophane noodles for her stir-fry dinner, which right now did not sound as delicious as anticipated. What if the board *did* finally resign to cutting salaries? She could probably make do; the cost of living in Dareville was not terribly high, and she could even go so far as finding a roommate to cut expenses if needed, but thinking about a smaller paycheck made her stomach churn. The imported noodles in her basket would be considered a luxury.

Ellie bit her lip, a habit when nervous. "If only we had some kind of rich benefactor, like colleges do." She looked at Lauren, who was browsing the boxes of rice for the one marked *low-carb*. "Any famous millionaire graduates of DPA willing to write us a check?"

"No. Not even an obscure millionaire. And all the rich people in Tidewater send their kids to Norfolk Academy or one of the Catholic schools over there."

"How about something more substantial, like a silent auction?" Ellie suggested. "We could get donations from around the area, like resort vacations and Norfolk Tides baseball tickets, and advertise everywhere. You know, we don't have to limit our fundraising to Dareville."

"We've thought about that," Lauren admitted, "but the consensus seems to be that outsiders are not going to want to give too much to a school to which they have no ties. I mean, it would be different if we were a high school or a college with an athletics program, but these are just kids who need a better school building. If the community around it is reluctant to fork over the cash, what makes you think people in Norfolk or Virginia Beach will?"

They turned a corner into the sauce and spice aisle. A pungent mixture of scents stung Ellie's nostrils. "If we had something everybody wanted, they'd give money, no matter what the cause is. It's all tax-deductible," she said. She had to remain hopeful; she really did not want to update her resume and look for work elsewhere, because she knew if the committee continued to come up empty-handed they would proceed to the final option—closing DPA altogether. The students would have to be bused into Suffolk to attend school, and she would have to make the dreaded commute into the larger, more populated areas of Tidewater to work. If she found work.

A gruff *ahem* prompted both ladies to look behind them. There stood Jake, smiling with a push-cart of seasonings he bottled himself, to replenish the empty spaces along the aisle shelves.

Ellie moved to one side. "I'm sorry, Jake. We were just chatting along, and we're in your way."

"Not at all, Ellie." Jake chuckled. "I was actually trying to get your attention. You do realize you're forgetting something very important that could help the school, don't you?"

Ellie could not think of what that would be. Her training was in elementary education, not business. The aforementioned bake sale was more her speed. "What's that?"

But Jake diverted his attention to Lauren now. She was watching Jake lean over his cart, a smitten grin plastered on her face. Ellie forced back the laugh bubbling in her throat. She knew Lauren had a thing for older men, and not only was the silver fox before them very attractive, but now available.

Actually, Ellie had to remind herself, probably not as such. Jake's wife had not been dead yet a year, and Ellie doubted the older man was ready for another relationship at the moment. She would not be surprised to learn, however, that the divorced and love-starved Lauren was counting the days until the requisite period of mourning was over for Jake.

The tiny glass vials of seasonings clinked together as the wheels of the cart jarred slightly from Jake's weight. "You know her cousin in New York is dating Brady Garriston, don't you?" he said to Lauren.

Lauren's eyes widened. "*Claire* is going out with Brady Garriston?" She punched Ellie in the shoulder, a bit too roughly for the jolt of pain coursing through Ellie's arm. "Why didn't you tell me? I *love* his music!"

Ellie felt her heart plummet through her intestines and simmer in her roiling stomach. Why did she tell *Jake* that? *When* did she tell Jake? She searched her mind for every minute conversation she had with grocer since Claire first told her, and for the life of her could not remember mentioning Brady at all. Clearly it must have slipped on a day she was not thinking, in a casual form of one-upmanship, maybe after Jake had bragged about one of his sons' many collegiate or professional achievements.

Given that nearly a month had passed since Claire broke it off with the singer, and was now dating somebody else, Ellie never saw fit to mention the relationship to anyone. She silently cursed Jake for having such a good memory, one much better than hers.

"Well," Ellie finally spoke, "I must have forgot. Besides, I don't really see what this has to do with saving DPA."

"It's relative if a certain somebody's cousin's famous boyfriend would consider a benefit concert for the school building fund." Jake's voice was innocent, yet clearly suggestive. Ellie looked at him in shock. Ask Brady Garriston to perform a show, after what Claire had done to him? Out of the question completely. Brady Garriston would no sooner reply to any message from a stranger in Dareville, Virginia than he would from a stalker, never mind that the stranger was Claire's relative. He was probably pissed off with Claire, so why do her any favors? Ellie did not even know how to get in touch with him, anyway.

She opened her mouth to express just that sentiment but was cut off by an exuberant Lauren. "Do you think he'd do that for us, El, if you got

Claire to ask him?"

"Well, you see, Lauren—"

"It's worth a shot," Jake said with a shrug. "These guys are always doing benefits like SARS Fest and Farm Aid, and it's always good publicity. Plus, if Claire and Brady are still as hot and heavy as you said they are, I'm sure he could be persuaded." Jake winked.

Ellie swallowed back the lump in her throat. Had she actually used those words, *hot and heavy?* Why could she not remember blabbing about Claire to Jake? Had she told anybody else and blocked it from her memory? "This is hardly Farm Aid, guys," Ellie pleaded, "it's an elementary school. And anyway—"

But Lauren had her by the shoulders. "Yeah, we know it's a long shot. These guys are always busy doing something, but if you don't shoot you've missed, right?" ·

Ellie melted at the glimmer of hope lighting Lauren's face, or maybe that was the flickering long bulb overhead creating the eerie glow. She set down her basket, not feeling hungry at all now.

"Just talk to Claire," Lauren said, stepping further down the aisle toward the checkout station. "If it's a dead end, at least we'll have tried something. I'll see you tomorrow. Bye, Jake." Lauren ducked away, and Ellie could have sworn the woman was skipping toward the registers. She was so dazed she had not heard Jake mutter a goodbye as he pushed the cart to the next aisle to finishing stocking product. Numbly she started toward the exit, leaving her groceries behind, still in the basket on the floor.

Me and my big mouth.

She felt relieved, however, that nobody else in Dareville knew how to contact Claire since she moved to her new building, so her transgressions here could be easily fixed. She took a deep breath. This was fixable, she knew. She would wait a few days and just tell Lauren that she called Claire and learned the two broke up, badly. *So sorry, there will be no benefit concert for the school. At least we tried, and I'll be at home baking cookies and Rice Krispies squares for the bake sale.*

The glass double doors slid open and Ellie padded into the gravel parking lot, feeling as if one weight had been lifted from her chest, only to be replaced with a heavier, more ungainly one. Yes, she should have said something off the bat about Claire, but Lauren and Jake had left her tongue-tied. Or was it because she did not want to look like a failure in front of them? Why would she feel that way, she wondered. She was not the one who dumped Brady Garriston. She had not had the opportunity to dump anybody in a long time.

Ellie let out a loud sigh and scanned the small lot for her brown Mazda. *Whatever*, she thought. The word was out, and she would have to fix everything. No big deal. Claire would never have to know this happened. It was not like they were in New York City now, and Brady Garriston was walking towards her...

Huh?

She stopped dead in her tracks.

Brady Garriston was walking towards her!

SIX

Newly settled Dareville, Virginia, resident Gary Stone, the artist formerly known as Brady Garriston, alighted from his leased Pontiac Firebird and started toward Jake's Organic Market. The real estate agent who had assisted him in signing the short-term rental agreement on a two-story cottage just inside the town's borders had recommended it as the only place to shop for groceries. Locally grown produce, a few imported goodies, and the best coffee this side of Starbucks, the plump, thirtyish woman had crowed. Everybody in Dareville shopped here, not to mention people traveling all the way from Suffolk and Smithfield.

So, too, would Gary Stone shop there. He desperately needed to stock his pantry, a fact evident by the rumbling in his stomach and the bare cupboard space in his new kitchen. Maybe he could get some of that coffee to sip as he shopped and quell the hunger, he hoped.

He was not five steps away from his car when he looked up and stumbled mid-stride, stopped by the pounding in his heart.

Claire?

Evidently his agent had neglected to tell him that aside from the people of Dareville, mirages of ex-girlfriends also shopped at Jake's, or least kept vigil outside the store. What was Claire doing here in this one-stoplight town? Had she followed him? Come to find him and ask him to come back to New York?

Impossible, he decided. Nobody knew he was here, not his ex-wife, not Cal, and not even Melissa, whom he had asked to oversee the care of his place in the city while he was away for the still undetermined period of time. She had agreed without suspicion, probably chalking up her father's behavior to a mid-life crisis of some sort.

He had told nobody in his circle of close friends that he was here, either, therefore Claire should never have known he had even left the city, but here she was in a wild floral print skirt, staring back at him in equal disbelief.

He thought his cock would stand at attention, and it could have had he not chosen to wear the tight-fitting black jeans he had on now. He wanted to run over to her and take her into a crushing embrace, and bury his face into those gorgeous tits, which looked absolutely appetizing in the scooped neck of her blouse.

Terrific. His cock fought its denim restraints. Surely the outline of an erection would soon be visible. In a parking lot full of people, too.

He forced his legs to move, but his feet felt as if they had been plunged into concrete shoes. Her electric gaze kept his voice from sounding. She looked so beautiful, lovelier now than during their last night together.

Man, but he wanted to plant her on the hood of the nearest car right now and fuck her like a horny teenager.

Instead he watched, dumbfounded, as she stepped closer to him with caution, and slowly the electricity dissolved into the humid air. He exhaled; this was not Claire, just another twin like One-Stoplight Sue from Knickerbocker's. Her face was sharper, her cheekbones higher, and her eyes a bit darker than Claire's green.

Still, she was gorgeous, like Sue. Did all women in Virginia look this hot? He shuddered to think what this Jake who owned the place would look like, should Brady ever get the chance to meet him.

The Claire clone pointed a trembling finger at him, her other hand pressed to her heart. "You," she said, her voice barely a whisper. "You-you're..."

Quickly he broke into her next words. "It's uncanny, isn't it?" He kept his voice smooth and innocent. This was not the first time he had to pull out this white lie in order to get some peace. "People say I look like him all the time, but I like to think *he* looks more like *me*."

Her face creased into a confused frown, and she managed to eke out, "Huh?"

"Brady Garriston," he said, nodding in question. "You were about to say that I was him, right?"

The woman appeared to regain some semblance of composure and straightened. "I did." He watched her eye him with open-mouthed awe. "I have so many of his CDs, and the resemblance is scary."

"Yeah, but we weren't separated at birth. I checked," Brady laughed, shoved his hands in his pockets, and rocked back on his heels. "So I won't be entitled to any inheritance soon." After a pregnant pause, punctuated by the growling in his stomach, he flashed her an apologetic smile. "Well, I need to get inside before all the good bananas are gone. Have a good day."

"Yeah, you, too." The woman waved lightly at his easy retreat, slowly, as if not of her own volition. He craned his neck back for another nod and faced forward, sighing inwardly with relief. Perhaps he should have rethought the part of the plan where he would roam through town looking as he did. Not everybody was going to be like One-Stoplight Sue, he realized, and not know him on sight. Maybe he would lighten his hair color, or just wear a ball cap and sunglasses in very public places.

Well, that would have to wait until he quelled his hunger. The doors of the grocery slid open to many fragrant aromas—fresh fruit, fresh coffee, and hot food from the small café set to one side. Not exactly the Carnegie Deli, but it would do just fine.

But he did not get even one foot over the threshold when that once babyish voice suddenly gained strength.

"Wait!" he heard her call.

* * *

The blood pounded in Ellie's ears; she could not hear her footsteps crunching through the gravel, or feel her legs as she rushed back toward the store to where the Brady Garriston look-alike stood. She could not let him walk in there, not while Lauren and Jake were still roaming the aisles. What if they saw him? They would react the same way she did, or perhaps worse, and maybe even accuse Ellie of holding out on them. He might not be so fortunate to get a word in edgewise with Lauren before being recruited to perform for some concert.

Not that Ellie had actually promised to deliver Brady Garriston for a benefit concert, but this poor guy did not need to get in the middle of the school's problems. If Lauren saw him, surely she would think Ellie had something to do with it.

She stopped and thought a moment. Maybe he was the type of guy who *would* be willing to involve himself in the school's problems. Maybe he was the charitable sort. Or was she that desperate to save the school, and save face, to say nothing of her job, to get him involved? To get him to commit fraud.

Come on, she scolded herself. *You just met the man. You don't know anything about him. You don't even know his name.*

"Wait!" she called again, and resumed her approach, a plan formulating in her mind.

The man paused and turned fully around to face her, his expression a mixture of amusement and curiosity. The doors slid shut behind him before he could enter.

"I...I know you're not you who I thought you were back there, just now." She hooked her thumb toward the parking lot, wanting to cry for sounding so silly. "But I've lived here a long time, and I feel I know just about everybody in town. I don't know you, though."

The man slowly nodded, and Ellie wondered if he thought she was hitting on him. That suspicion deepened as his lips curled into an appreciative smile and his gaze swept her skirt and peasant shirt, which she realized hugged her a bit too tightly and accentuated her full breasts. No wonder the school principal, Mr. Yost, had greeted her with such disapproval this morning at work. This was not the appropriate dress for an elementary school teacher, she could hear the stodgy old man saying.

"Gary Stone," the man said, and offered his hand. It was a large hand with long, manicured fingers, the kind that could easily have found a home caressing a piano keyboard. It nearly swallowed her own as Ellie reciprocated the greeting.

Her entire body warmed to the touch. She saw those hands caressing a keyboard, then caressing a woman's body, her body. Circling her waist and sliding upward to cup her breasts, rolling her nipples between those strong fingers. Bringing them closer to his face so he could lave each one tenderly with his tongue...

Down, girl. She pressed her thighs together to conceal the dampness she was certain would soon be trickling down her leg.

For all the time passed since Claire dumped the real Brady Garriston, the fantasies Ellie had harbored also faded into oblivion. Now they bubbled back to the surface. Why did this man have to look so much like him? Why did he have to release his grip?

"And you are correct," he was saying, and Ellie snapped to attention. "I recently moved here from New York."

"New York City?" Ellie brightened. "I have a cousin who lives there. Of course, I wouldn't expect you to know her. I mean, there's got to be, what, seven or eight million people living in New York? What are the odds that you might know *her*?" She was babbling and could not seem to stop; she felt suddenly silly and frightened. Gary Stone was going to think she was a loon, that maybe all of Dareville was like her.

"I don't know, strangers things have happened," Gary said with a laugh, but Ellie could easily see the discomfort on his face. She was spooking him, and he clearly wanted to bolt for the safety of the grocery store. In fact, his foot had depressed the trigger to reopen the doors, revealing the activity from within the store.

"Uh." Ellie peered over his shoulder and spotted Lauren chatting with a checkout girl while digging through her purse. The woman had not spotted them, yet. Instinctively, Ellie grasped Gary by the arm and guided him away from the registers.

"What are you doing?" Gary asked, taken aback, but thankfully he did nothing to wrest away from Ellie.

"Well, seeing as how you're new in town and all, I thought you might like a tour of Jake's," she said, and pulled him toward a stand about to avalanche with various types of apples.

Gary turned back to the entrance, and Ellie held back a gasp as his face momentarily became visible from the point of view of anybody at the checkout station. "Shouldn't we get a cart or something first?" he said, pointing to the corral. "I have quite a lot to buy. I don't think I can carry it all."

"Oh, there's usually an orphaned one idling somewhere in the dry goods aisle, don't worry." She held out her free hand in a show model's gesture. "Now this is one of Jake's many produce displays," she said, trying her best to ignore the look of bewilderment on Gary Stone's face. He still looked too much like Brady, regardless of how his brows creased. "As you can see, Jake offers a wide variety of apples. You got your Macintoshes, Red Delicious, Granny Smith…"

Gary stepped warily away from her. "Yes, we have apples in New York, too, uh…" He snapped his fingers, and Ellie let out an embarrassed laugh.

"Oh, God. I'm sorry. My name's Ellie Shaw." She quick-stepped to his other side to block the view from the checkout station, then cast a worried glance in that direction. How long did it take for Lauren to buy groceries? Was she telling the clerk the story of her life over there? "You must think I'm some kind of lunatic, dragging you all over a grocery store without telling you my name."

"Well, you've only dragged me about fifty feet, which I suppose would seem sane for a small town like this. But now that I know your name, my opinion hasn't changed much." But Gary's tone softened as Ellie cast her eyes downward. "Oh, I'm sorry," he quickly added, "I didn't mean it to sound like that. I guess I'm just not used to being accosted by people in public. You don't see much of that in New York City." He then lifted a shoulder in a tired shrug. "Actually, I shouldn't say that, either. I'm sure people have been accosted in the city, though I doubt all the experiences are this pleasant."

Ellie looked up at him, warming to the compliment. His smile nearly made her forget that she was not talking to Brady Garriston, and what a smile he had. He resembled any, if not all, of the CD covers in her collection. Such nice lips, she noticed. She would not have minded those lips on hers, or anywhere on her body.

She saw those lips nestled between her thighs, rubbing against her pussy, pursed against her clit and driving her to distraction.

Stop it. She had to think of something else before her wild imagination caused her to orgasm right in the middle of the produce section. Sure, Jake's stock was good, but not *that* good.

"Really?" She bit her lip. "You've never been accosted in the Big Apple? Not even for looking like a famous singer?"

"Hm? Oh, yeah, the Brady thing." Gary chuckled. "Well, living in New York has its advantages. Famous people walk around all the time and aren't bothered."

"Oh, man, if I ever got to New York I'd probably go nuts if I saw somebody famous."

"I don't know. You seemed pretty composed

earlier."

"Yeah, but that was—" Ellie stopped. She did not want to get into the whole story of Brady and Claire and Lauren's ideas. "Nothing, it was nothing."

She heard the doors *whoosh* open, and watched Lauren exit, her arms laden with paper sacks. At the far end of the store, she spied Jake slipping through a door leading to storage. Other shoppers glided past without a second look at them. Gary would be fine in the store by himself, she decided.

"You'll have to forgive me," she said finally. "I'm acting a bit crazy because of work problems. Not that I hate my job, I love it to death, but there's a chance I could lose it, or be forced to take a pay cut, which means I might have to quit and find something that pays just as much or more but I like less." She was babbling again, and Gary was eyeing her with such amusement that Ellie felt the heat rise to her face.

"You know what?" she added, backing away. "You're not interested in my problems. I'm just going to wish you a good day and leave you to shop in peace, because I don't want you to think we're all like this here, a bunch of babbling loons."

But Gary shook his head and offered a complacent smile. "No, you don't have to go. Look over there." True to Ellie's earlier word, an orphaned cart came rolling listlessly toward them from an aisle, as if being pushed by a ghost. "Seems fate has destined us to this cart," he said.

Ellie smirked. "Fate is not without a sense of

humor. We *would* be given the one cart with the bum wheel." She pointed to the wheel in question, which appeared to be stuck in an askew position, different than the others.

Her heart stopped. She had said *we*, as if they were a couple. What must he have thought of that? Soon she would graduate from apple stands to china patterns and send this guy screaming back to New York City for a bit of normalcy!

To her relief, he appeared unfazed by the slip. "Oh, it'll work fine. Watch this." He grasped the handlebar and bounced the cart twice, dislodging the wheel from its stuck position, then pushed the cart back and forth in a test run. "It's all in the wrist."

"Indeed it is," Ellie said in appreciation. And Gary Stone had really nice wrists, and arms and shoulders, taut and strong in a short-sleeved shirt that pulled tightly across his chest as he arched his back and turned the cart in the opposite direction. He filled out that pair of black jeans nicely, too, she noticed, admiring the convex curve of the zipper hiding more of Gary Stone that she would not mind seeing.

Did the real Brady Garriston look this good up close? Was he this charming? If so, Claire was an idiot for letting go such a fine specimen of man.

"You okay?" he asked her suddenly, concerned.

"Hm?" The tangy aroma of fresh fruit, coupled with her sudden bout of lust, made her nauseated, and she realized she had been swaying as if about to faint. "Oh, I'm fine. I just really, *really* like shopping here." *So much I could come just staring at the cucumbers. They're not just for breakfast anymore.*

Lord, if she could have sounded any sillier…

She watched him select a few apples from the Granny Smith pyramid and drop them into a flimsy plastic bag, tying a knot instead of using a twist tie. "Since you're here, why don't you show me around the rest of the store?" he suggested. "I'm going to be shopping here often, and it wouldn't hurt to have a guide to give me the inside dirt on what's fresh and what's to be avoided." He winked at her and sent her heart rate speeding. She had never seen Brady Garriston wink, but imagined Gary did it the same way. Add those nice gray eyes to the already growing list of favorite body parts.

She did not feel her hands take the bare spot of the cracked cart handle Gary left as he slid to one side. Together they pushed the cart through the aisle she had previously vacated.

"You were right about the carts, but looks like you neglected to mention baskets." Gary crooked his neck forward to the basket Ellie had left behind at the far end of the aisle. Her groceries were still inside.

"Huh?" Ellie tried to sound surprised as they moved closer. "Look at that. Can you believe some people?" She hoped nobody had seen her leave it on the floor, and she quick-stepped ahead of the cart to retrieve the abandoned goods. "I should put these things back. Jack doesn't like for the stock to be out of place. Messes up his inventory count."

"Looks like somebody wanted stir fry and changed his mind," Gary observed as Ellie rifled through the crinkling plastic packages. "That actually sounds good, though, and here I don't have to go looking for everything to make it." He looked at her. "What about you? Up for a tour of my new kitchen and some stir-fry tonight? I think I unpacked the wok."

He then frowned. "Then again, I can't remember packing a wok in the first place, don't recall ever owning one. There wouldn't happen to be a Williams Sonoma store around here, would there?"

"Please." Ellie laughed. Now *he* was babbling. What had she done to him? "Closest one is in Virginia Beach about an hour away. You *really* have to want stir fry to travel that far."

"I suppose a spaghetti pot would work. I mean, it's mostly noodles, right?"

Ellie swallowed, her heart pounding in her temples. A vision of Gary standing before a stove, in nothing but an apron reading *Kiss the Cook*, flashed before her eyes. Oh, she would like to kiss this cook.

"Or," she said, holding the basket close to her, "since I already have a wok, you could come over to my place and I'll cook. Think of it as a Welcome to Dareville dinner."

"Sounds daring." His voice turned husky. "I'd love to."

Damn, he even sounded like Brady Garriston, from what she could discern through listening to her CDs. She imagined that same deep voice whispering sweet nothings in Claire's ear, then her own.

She would not have minded hearing some not-so-sweet nothings from Gary Stone, either. Maybe a deep-throated, orgasmic cry as he lay pinned underneath her.

Did I just ask this guy to my apartment? Her body went numb.

As they sauntered around the corner to the next aisle, conferring over directions and time, Ellie tried to focus on the man before her, and not the one in her mind. *This is not Brady, this is just some guy,* she kept telling herself. *Some really gorgeous guy. Some total stranger I just invited over to my house, who's probably a serial killer on the lam and whose MO is to murder young blonde women...*

No. She had to stop thinking like that. She was watching too many cop shows. He seemed like a nice guy, and anybody who could put up with her scatterbrained observations for more than a minute had to have a heart of gold.

Let him have a cock of steel, too.

Down, girl!

Before she knew it, they had traversed the entire store, and Gary's cart was full. "End of the line," Gary announced, and gently eased the package of Chinese noodles from Ellie's grasp. She had not realized she was clinging to it like a life preserver. "Let me get the groceries, since you're going through the trouble of cooking tonight. Take what you need home and I'll be over later, maybe split a bottle of wine beforehand."

"Hm? Sure, that would be great." Ellie surrendered the noodles and watched carefully as the clerk slid each item from Gary's cart across the lit scanner. The young girl moved with fluid disinterest and not once looked up at either of them. Ellie wondered if a girl so young would know who Brady Garriston was, and decided they would be safe from another mistaken identity pronouncement.

A few silent minutes later, Gary had swiped his credit card in the proper slot, and Ellie had a bag full of the necessary ingredients for dinner. "I guess I better get moving, then," she said, stepping away from the register. "I need to straighten up the house and feed the cat. You're not allergic, are you?"

Gary was returning the credit card to his billfold. "Long as she doesn't bite," he said with a smile that implied he would not mind if Ellie bit. It threw her off guard and she let loose a nervous laugh.

"Wonderful. See you at seven, then." And she wobbled out of the store on rubber legs, hoping Gary was not monitoring her exit, and asking herself what in the hell had she just done. Wondering if Gary Stone would turn out to be anything like his famous clone, and whether that was a good or bad thing.

SEVEN

"El, you don't need my permission," Claire groaned on the other end of the line. At least, it sounded like a groan to Ellie. Since Claire was on her cell phone, though, it could have been static prickling her ear as her receiver was pinned with her shoulder.

"Just have a good time. You're allowed to do that every now and then, and you should do it more often," Claire was saying, the static now an inaudible blur, muffled by the noise made as Ellie plunged into a silverware drawer looking for two forks and two knives of the same pattern. So far she was three quarters of the way to a matching set.

"I wasn't asking your permission, you know that." Ellie had asked her cousin if she was crazy to invite a strange man to her apartment for dinner, but of course she should have known to expect Claire to tease her. Stranger things, no doubt, must happen in the big city all the time, like people getting married within five minutes of meeting.

Wild, animal sex within five minutes of meeting Gary Stone, now, Ellie would have welcomed. But not at the cost of her life if he did turn out to be a serial killer.

"He's not a serial killer," Claire said in reassurance as Ellie voiced that concern. "Serial killers don't stalk small towns where they're more likely to be caught."

"There's a vote of confidence," Ellie muttered, and found the last matching piece of flatware. She shut the drawer with her hip. She did not mention that Gary was the spitting image of Brady Garriston, as she was not certain if that would upset Claire.

"Jeez, how long has it been since you went out on a date, anyway?" Claire asked.

"Too damn long. I guess it's partly my fault for living in a town where the most eligible bachelor can still remember the day he met President Eisenhower, when the man was still a lowly general." Ellie grimaced and held up the black-handled knife. What was that green stain on the blade? She hoped it would come out before Gary arrived.

"How is Grandpa, by the way?"

"Very funny. Yeesh, one set of cousins marries, and the whole town gets a reputation."

"What about Jake, Jr.?" Claire pointed out. "He's a nice-looking guy, as I recall. His dad's not so bad looking, either."

"J.J. lives at the beach now, and Lauren would kill me if I made a move on Jake." She tossed the offending knife in the sink and plucked a cleaner white-handled one off the counter. "Hey, you think he'll notice if the flatware doesn't match?"

"If you had married Arnie Logan like we wanted you to, you'd have Grandma Minnie's entire wedding set," Claire aped in a perfect representation of Ellie's mother, then cackled.

"If *I* had married Arnie Logan, I wouldn't be fixing dinner for another man, and Arnie wouldn't care if we ate with our hands."

"If I had married Arnie Logan, I'd leave him a TV dinner in the oven have the other man take me someplace nice. Arnie wasn't my type." Claire lapsed back into Ellie's mother's voice. "He was perfect for you, however."

"Don't," Ellie warned, and stretched the phone cord across the kitchen so she could set the flatware on her small dinner table with the plates she had selected for tonight. "How am I supposed to have a good time if I keep hearing Mom's voice nagging at me?" She reminded herself to turn off the phone ringer when Gary arrived; Ellie's mother seemed to have a sixth sense about her daughter where her romantic life—or lack thereof—was concerned. Chances were high Mrs. Shaw would call tonight to extricate details before either one of them could enjoy the first bite of dinner.

"Why *didn't* you marry Arnie, anyway?" Claire asked. "He seemed kind of sweet on you."

"Arnie was sweet. It just happens I prefer men with all their teeth. And this guy," Ellie rolled her eyes, "oh, he's got a nice set."

"What about the rest of him? What's he look like?"

Ellie returned to the kitchen and paused, her hand clutching a cabinet door. "He's, uh, very good looking. New in town, I already told you that. Short, dark hair, kinda dark eyes. Nice build, too. I think he must bike or something. He doesn't look like a body builder or anything like that. I'd say he's a few years older than me, too."

"Maybe you'll know for certain tonight, maybe a bit more than just his age," Claire purred.

Don't I wish. The apron fantasy returned full force, only now the apron was much smaller and reworded to read *Kiss the Cock.*

Ellie quickly regained her composure. "It's dinner, Claire. He's going to come over, we're going to eat, maybe talk a while, and after that he's going home. Honestly," Ellie sighed. "I have no interest in what's underneath his clothes and whether or not he works out."

Liar.

She retrieved two wineglasses from the cabinet, then returned one with a small chip in the rim. All she had thought about since leaving Jake's was Gary, in and out of his clothes. She recalled especially his arms, and how his muscles bulged against the sleeves of his shirt, and as she cooked dinner she could think of nothing but how those same arms would feel wrapped around her, lifting her to carry her to bed.

"Liar," Claire sneered.

Quickly Ellie spun around to the stove to check on the stir-fry. It sizzled in the wok, and Ellie carelessly tossed around the ingredients with a wooden spatula. She had to change the subject, and fast; her body temperature was close to surpassing the heat of the stove. "So," she said, "what do you have planned for tonight?"

"Robert and I are going out for drinks later," Claire said, and Ellie could detect a note of reluctance in her cousin's voice. Had she grown tired of

this guy already? Robert was her third love interest since breaking it off with Brady several weeks
ago. At this rate there would be no more men in
the city Claire had not yet dated. She would have
to start on New Jersey soon.

"You don't sound too thrilled."

"Well, he wants to go to Knickerbocker's,
and I don't, because that's sort of where Brady
hangs out with his musician friends." A heavy
sigh roared through the receiver. "What if we run
into him there?"

"You get up and go somewhere else. There's a
million restaurants in New York," Ellie said, but
her body language defied the cool tone she used
over the phone. She had to wonder if Claire's recent string of brief relationships was tied to Brady,
and whether or not Claire regretted dumping him.
She had talked with Claire about five or six times
since that night Claire announced Brady's return
to the city, and each time there was a sighing Brady
reference. We were driving to Long Island and
one of Brady's songs came on the radio. I missed
my stop on the subway because I thought I saw
Brady and didn't want to get off there. There's a
huge replica of Brady floating over Macy's in the
Thanksgiving parade this year. Ellie did not doubt
that Claire still had feelings for the man, but trying
to get Claire to admit it was not likely.

And in less than fifteen minutes, his dop-
pelganger was due at her apartment. Maybe she
should say something, Ellie mused to herself, if
only to light a fire under her cousin. She adjusted
the phone against her shoulder for a more com-

fortable grip and turned off the stove.

Nah, best to be direct. "You know what? Maybe you guys should go to that place. Maybe Brady will be there, and you'll realize how bad you still have it for him. If he's still pining for you, you'll have a chance to make up for lost time."

"Ellie, I do not—"

But Ellie cut her off. "Do you?" she posed. "You claim not to care for him, yet every time I talk to you his name comes up."

"I never said I didn't care about him anymore, it's just that I don't want to be in a relationship with him. We're not..." Ellie heard Claire's voice drift. "You know what? I'll just leave you to your dinner, and don't worry about anything. Go easy on the hoisin sauce and don't do anything I wouldn't do."

"That's a rather long list, more like a phone book," Ellie said, but Claire had rung off too soon and missed the jibe at her expense.

* * *

Ellie's garden apartment was situated at one corner of small brick building, housing five other dwellings. Her immediate next door neighbor, like Ellie, had a large picture window near her front door, which might have granted Brady full view of a stranger's living room had the blinds not been closed. Instead, as he ambled up the sidewalk to Ellie's door, he was treated to three pairs of curious, juvenile eyes, all peering between crooked slats, watching his every move. Brady offered a slight nod to acknowledge their presence, and they quickly vanished.

He had to chuckle at that, imagining he must have provided Ellie's neighbor children with the first great mystery of their lives—to learn the identity of the strange man coming up to walk to meet the nice lady next door. Neighbors in New York City were no less curious. He remembered similar scenes during his salad days in lower-income brownstones shared with others, only those people were a bit more blatant in satisfying their curiosity.

Ellie's front door was decorated with a wreath of pink and white silk flowers and spray, a fitting decoration for a woman of Ellie's demeanor. She had been so bubbly and extroverted in the grocery store, and very attractive. It made some sense for him to initially mistake her for Claire in the parking lot, for she resembled the other woman in behavior as well as looks.

So very attractive. He had not been able to get her off his mind since leaving the grocery store. How much like Claire could she be? Was she as straight-laced in the sack? Could she be uninhibited? Would he ever find out for himself?

He hitched up the waist of his jeans to stifle the threatening erection. The drive to Ellie's apartment had been no more comfortable, with thoughts of Ellie's ripe, naked body writhing against his in a tangled, horizontal dance.

Calm down, he warned himself. This woman might actually have invited him for dinner, to have dinner, and nothing more.

More could come at a later time, though.

No. He was not going to turn back into a raging horndog, he had promised himself that. Since that night with Jared, he had behaved himself, had not masturbated once, and had not actively sought company of either sex. To be certain, he could easily have had the real estate agent who led him to his cottage. She had given off plenty of signs.

The whole point of coming to this town was to renew himself, write more songs, become a new man.

God, but he was horny, though.

He tightened his grip on the bottle of wine brought with him and shook his head. This woman was not Claire. Claire was in New York. This woman was Ellie Shaw, a nice Dareville woman with whom he was going have dinner, a glass or two of wine, some animated conversation, nothing more. He was not going do anything stupid. As small as Dareville was, Brady feared a bit of hometown gossip could go a long way, and Ellie claimed to know everybody. What would stop her from reporting him through the grapevines were he to make a move she didn't welcome? He didn't have the energy or desire to start over again in a new town.

No, just dinner. Then he'd go home and tinker around on the piano, try out some lyrics that had been brewing in the back of his mind for the past few days. Maybe a relaxing evening with a lovely young woman would help dislodge his block, he decided, ringing the doorbell.

A blowjob would have been better than dinner, though.

Brady fought to expel the image from his mind as the door flew open.

Ellie's greeting was as breathless and askew as her appearance. Her hair was mussed, and dark sauce stained the red apron she wore over her clothes, which she had not changed since their meeting at Jake's. Still, she was very pretty, more so when her face broke into a wide grin.

"Come in. Everything's almost ready. Except me, I'm a mess." She waved Brady inside and gladly took the proffered bottle of wine. "This looks lovely, thank you." She inspected the label, then frowned. "You'll have to forgive me, though. I'm an absolute dunce when it comes to wine. I know it comes in red and white, but this…"

"That," Brady pointed to the label as he was ushered into the living room, "is plum wine. Normally one would have it with Japanese, but it's the closest I could find at that little liquor store just over the county line." Unconsciously he hooked a thumb over his shoulder as if to indicate the location of the store.

Ellie laughed and pointed in the opposite direction, toward her sliding glass patio doors. "Actually, I know the store and it's more that way," she said, and brought the bottle to her galley kitchen. "I'm surprised you found something this fancy there. Even though this is a dry county, people mainly go there for beer."

Brady lifted one shoulder in a listless half-shrug. "I shudder to think how long that particular bottle's been there, then," he replied, grinning. "Let's hope plum wine ages well like the rest."

"Looks like it should be chilled. I'll put it in the fridge 'til it's time to eat." Ellie waved to the sofa from the kitchen. "Make yourself at home."

"Thanks." Brady took his time getting to the sofa, first sauntering though a self-guided tour of Ellie's living room. Her homespun décor, coupled with worn, outdated furniture, spoke clearly of an owner whose yearly salary barely matched what he had earned from sales of his first hit single alone.

Still, her apartment was cozy and comfortable, accented with the proper feminine touches. There were two wrought-iron sconces above either end of the sofa, each holding a scented candle, fashion magazines arranged in a fan pattern on the coffee table, and painted ceramic picture frames encasing photos of loved ones, arranged on a bookshelf with several romance novels.

He sat at one end of the sofa, and his eye caught the latest copy of a celebrity gossip magazine, folded back to a page filled with blind items, resting on the arm. Many appeared easily solvable, but one in particular caught his eye:

Could it be that a Rock and Roll Hall of Fame hopeful with a reputation with the ladies also dabbles on the flip side? A young friend of ours recently told us of his one-night, sold-out performance with this rock-hard legend, and you can bet his story is certainly hotter than anything on the charts right now.

Jared. Brady shook his head and smiled. Could this have been about him? If so, he hoped at the very least Jared was paid well for his tip, and was relieved to see that the blind item columnist had not guessed him but a number of other, more obvious singers.

He set the magazine aside and stood, and murmured to Ellie the expected compliments about her home and studied the photos, all of which featured Ellie posing with people he assumed were family. There was Ellie sandwiched by an older couple, probably her parents, in the foreground of an amusement park, Ellie with the same cat he had seen following her mistress into the kitchen, and Ellie with a striking blonde woman in sunglasses who could have been a dead ringer for…

Claire?

He coughed.

Ellie's head poked around the corner of the kitchen. "Did you say something?"

Brady felt his heart stop. Had he said Claire's name out loud? Had Ellie heard? His head snapped toward Ellie, and he smiled complacently. "Uh," he stammered as she waited, "no, I was just looking at your shelf. There's quite a few good pictures of you here."

He cringed and wondered if what he said sounded sillier to her than it had to him as the words issued past his tied tongue. Thankfully, Ellie only shrugged and said, "Yeah, I come from a big family, and everybody thinks they're Annie Leibowitz the way they're always popping flashbulbs in my face." She crooked her neck toward the small dining table opposite the kitchen in its own alcove, set for dinner. "Have a seat. I'll have the food over in a sec."

"Sounds good," Brady said, but nothing sounded good, or smelled good. The aroma of stir-fried vegetables and noodles caused his stomach to roil, and the anxiety he now felt did little to assuage matters. What was Ellie Shaw doing in a photograph with Claire? Were they sisters? Claire had never mentioned a sister, but they certainly looked enough alike. What were the odds of that happening?

Moreover, what were the odds that he would slip up again and call Ellie by Claire's name? If the two were indeed related, surely Claire would have mentioned· to Ellie that she was dating, or had dated, a famous singer.

He took the chair opposite Ellie's, facing the mirrored wall of the alcove, just as she served him a steaming plate of stir-fry and indicated the various sauce bottles on the table for his use. He waited for her to fetch the wine and take her chair before eating and resuming conversation, which Ellie dominated gaily with punctuated laughter and anecdotes about her job.

He needed to stay focused on her, he knew, and not slip. Otherwise, Ellie might realize he truly was Brady Garriston, and possibly think the worst of him. If Claire had indeed talked about him, she could have said anything, blamed him for their breakup, and made him out to be some kind of pervert or loser. He could not let that happen. He liked Ellie.

He nodded as she talked, and caught his reflection in the mirror behind her. He still had done nothing to alter his appearance, and he wondered if eventually he should reveal his true self to her. If she was as close to Claire as the photo indicated, perhaps Ellie could provide the key to his getting back into Claire's good graces.

Yeah, he thought. Befriending Ellie would work to his advantage. He would let some time lapse as they got to know each other better, and he would confide in her his secret, with no mention of Claire at all. Ellie would see how he really was, how serious he was about his music, and perhaps pass along her observations to Claire.

Maybe Claire would change her mind about him.

He took another bite of dinner; it was starting to taste better.

EIGHT

Oh. My. God.

Ellie put a hand to her chest and tried to keep her heart from bursting free.

He knew Claire, he had recognized her photo and said her name aloud.

Gary knew Claire, and did not think Ellie had heard his awkward cry of surprise. The man now roaming around her apartment, about to sit down at her table, eat her dinner, on her good china, was not Gary Stone.

He was Brady Garriston. It *had* to be him.

Now the pounding traveled south. Her other hand went to her crotch to still the fluttering. Ellie wanted to slap her head. Gary Stone—*Garriston*. It made perfect sense.

A famous rock singer, a man she had fantasized about, dreamed of fucking, was in her home!

She picked up the serving bowl of stir fry with trembling hands. Her mood suddenly fell. What the hell was Brady Garriston doing in Dareville, Virginia, of all places, using an assumed name? Was this some sick plan to make conquest of every woman in her family, and she happened to be next on the list after Claire? Was he planning a trip to Daytona, Florida after this to nail her mother?

No. Ellie plunged a serving fork into the bowl. That could not be it. Gary's, rather Brady's, presence here had to be mere coincidence. He seemed like such a nice guy, and Ellie doubted Claire would have mentioned her or Dareville to him during the brief time they dated. Ellie was aware that as a lawyer working for a prestigious New York firm, Claire wanted to distance herself as much as possible from her small-town ties, her relationship with Ellie excluded. She would never have said anything to Brady.

That still did not answer the question of how he ended up here, though. Could be he was trying to escape the drudgery of celebrity in the big city. Many of the entertainment magazines Ellie read reported on movie stars relocating to remote towns in Idaho and Montana for peace and quiet. Dareville would surely fit the bill for somebody wanting to get away from the bustle of the Big Apple.

Or, maybe losing Claire was the reason for this drastic move. Maybe he was so distraught over being dumped that, after being turned down again after coming back from Europe, he decided to start all over again in a new town as a different person. That sounded plausible as well, given Claire's assessment of Brady's behavior.

If so, how romantic was that? Ellie nearly swooned at the stove.

She watched as Gary—dare she even think of him as Brady?—took a chair. His jeans pulled tightly over his thighs and accentuated his taut waist as he sat up straight. Those incredible hands folded in his lap, hiding the bulge in his crotch. Even his simple act of sitting down to dinner made her horny.

"Smells good," he called from the table. Ellie started, nearly dropping the bowl. Damn, but he had a sexy, deep voice! It sounded much better in person than on his CDs. She had thought his voice sexy when he was Gary Stone, but now...

Quickly she composed herself enough to walk the few steps to the dining area and portioned out the stir-fry on their plates. "Thanks," she said in a half-giggle. "I haven't tried out the wok in a while, I hope everything turned out okay."

She leaned close into him as she doled out the vegetable and noodle mix. She felt his eyes on her; his cologne tickled her senses. Claire had slept with this man. He was famous. She had his entire music catalogue on a wire rack not ten feet away. He was gorgeous. She had not been with a man in *so* long.

She wanted to clear the table with one dramatic sweep of her arm, hoist herself on the table, and really give him something to eat.

Instead, she calmly set the serving bowl in the space between their place settings. "Oh," she said innocently. "Let me get the wine." With that, she dashed to the refrigerator and opened the door, effectively blocking herself from his viewpoint.

The blast of cold air felt good on her skin, but did little to quell the heat pooling inside her, making her pussy ache. How was she going to get through dinner without calling his bluff? Worse yet, without blurting out that she wanted to fuck him?

Calm down. She reached for the wine bottle and paused. Would she be acting this way if he really were plain old Gary Stone? Of course, she had not thought Gary plain originally, but this added twist definitely intrigued her, and turned her on.

It turned her on so much that she quickly undid her bra and pulled it from the neck of her blouse, then hiked up her skirt and removed her panties. Stuffing them in the empty vegetable crisper, she grabbed the bottle and pressed it to one nipple, then the other, to harden them. She felt free and dangerous with nothing restraining her tender spots.

She wondered exactly how much further she could go. Maybe the wine she held would help.

* * *

"So what brings you to a place like Dareville?" she asked as the conversation hit a lull. They had talked about her job for the most part, but Ellie decided she had better stop. Elementary school anecdotes didn't seem to make for good pretense to foreplay. "Seems like you could go anywhere in the world if you wanted."

Brady chuckled. "Not exactly. I do have some money put away, but I'm hardly well off to the point of living the life of luxury."

"I see." Clearly he did not want to expose his ruse. Ellie had read enough celebrity magazines to know Brady Garriston did quite well for himself, thank you.

She took another sip of wine and winced.

Gary/Brady had warned her it would not taste like any red wine, but the effect seemed the same. She felt giddy all over.

Stealthily she rubbed the glass over one nipple that appeared to have softened, then thrust her shoulders back to make the protrusion more prominent. Brady happened to look up at this moment, and Ellie relished the bemused look on his face as he nearly choked on his dinner.

She batted her eyelashes. "Do you need some more water?"

Brady pressed a fist to his mouth and shook his head. He kept his gaze fixed on her breasts. Good boy.

He recovered and she asked what he did for a living. "You probably won't believe me when I tell you this, given my resemblance to you-know-who," Brady faltered, and set down his fork, "but I am a musician."

"Really?" Ellie raised her eyebrows. This was going to be interesting.

"A studio musician, actually. Working behind the scenes with other recording artists. All the work and none of the glory, I suppose." Brady looked down at his now empty plate. "There's a studio in Virginia Beach, where I'm going to be working for the next few months, making a record. Pay's not bad, and I get away from the city for awhile."

"Is anybody famous going to be recording here in Virginia?" *Besides you, I'm assuming?* Ellie poured herself more wine and pointed the bottle toward Brady. He tipped his glass closer and she refilled it.

"I'm not at liberty to say," Brady replied, winking. "One reason people like to use this particular studio is because of the anonymity. They like to move around town without being seen."

"Makes sense. I don't think I'd want to be constantly hounded for autographs everywhere I went." As for being seen, that she very much wanted.

She half-rose from her seat under the pretense of clearing the table. Reaching for a salt shaker placed purposely on the edge of the table, she flicked her wrist and sent it tumbling to the ground, where it rolled to their feet.

Brady scooted his chair back an inch. "Don't move. I'll get it," he said, and ducked under the linen cloth.

You most certainly will, Ellie thought. Her heart thrumming double time, she inched her rear to the edge of her seat, spread her knees far apart, and hiked her skirt to her thighs. If all went according to plan, Brady Garriston would have an eye level view of her slick, shaved pussy. Dessert.

She waited, then smiled as a thunderous *thud* from below vibrated the tabletop, rattling condiment bottles and flatware. Seconds later, Brady's head emerged slowly from the other end. He was clutching the salt shaker, and gently set it down next to his plate. The look on his face was unreadable: mainly surprise, but Ellie detected some uncertainty. She wanted to laugh out loud, and hope for that as some kind of compliment.

"Here you go," he said.

She maintained her poker face and settled back into her chair. "Save room for dessert?"

"Dessert?" Brady's bewildered expression did not change. Dessert appeared to be the farthest thing from his mind. If he only knew.

"What's for dessert?"

Ellie took the pepper shaker that rested near her other hand and tossed it under the table.

"I'll give you a hint, it's where you left it."

* * *

I had to ask.

Ellie could not have been subtler smashing the wok upside his head.

Calmly he pressed his palms on the table and matched her coy smile. "Pepper doesn't seem like an appropriate spice to have with dessert, you think?"

And Ellie bit her lip again. He had thought that charming in the grocery store. Now, she appeared very much the vixen. Not that he was complaining.

Or should he? This was supposed to be just a dinner date. He was going to behave himself. He was not going to act like a horndog, and prove his maturity, and hopefully have this woman help him do that. He had not expected this.

Now he wondered if that emergency condom was still tucked in that one flap of his billfold.

Her bite softened, and the tip of her tongue poked through her lips. No, he was not complaining, but was very close to forgetting what's-her-name. The old Brady was never going to go away.

The world would not let that happen, and he had to resign himself to that.

No, he was *definitely* not complaining.

"Depends on how hot you like things, I suppose," came her reply.

"Touché. But, if you ask me, I don't think anything needs to be added." Brady edged his chair back some more and settled one hand on his crotch, stroking the growing bulge straining underneath the tight denim. "My compliments on the presentation as well."

He watched her shift around in her chair, his heartbeat increasing as he stole a glance under the tablecloth. Her knees lifted and spread even farther apart, almost 180 degrees. Did this woman practice yoga? It certainly would be a treat to fuck her with her legs wrapped around his neck.

He grinned. She was all but erecting a neon sign of an arrow pointing south, and here he was with what surely must have looked to her to be a stupid grin on his face, doing nothing.

Except trying to masturbate through his jeans.

Then, as if reading his mind, she asked, "Waiting for something?"

"You have to ask?" Without another thought, he sank to the floor and inched closer to Ellie's chair, rolling the errant pepper shaker out of the way. She was stroking her pussy now, playing with the folds and prying them apart to give him full view of her slick opening. One finger massaged her clit while another dipped in and out of that moist opening, then beckoned him closer.

He was going to explode in his pants, he just knew it.

Instead he kept that thought at bay, hoping at some point Ellie would want to reciprocate, and enjoy dessert as well. His hands bracing the edge of the wooden seat, he dipped forward and laved a trail upward from the lower edge of her slit to the top of her cleft. He looked up as she moaned, and saw that Ellie's blouse had quickly been shed; her hands now massaged her bare breasts and pinched her thick, dark pink nipples.

She looked down at him with a wicked gleam in her eyes. "Not to your liking?" she asked, teasing.

"I like it fine." He sighed. How stupid did that sound? He *loved* it. He could not believe how long he had let himself go without it.

But he could not take his eyes off of those luscious, full breasts being so expertly kneaded. Every inch of her body looked so delicious. "I'm just wondering if I'd enjoy sucking on one of those tits more."

But Ellie pointed him back to her pussy. "Finish dessert and we'll see."

"Yes, ma'am." And he tucked back into her, lapping at her folds until his tongue finally touched her clit, which he tapped in a circular motion very slowly. Ellie writhed in place, and released one of her breasts to clasp a hand against the back of Brady's head. He did not notice, but was too entranced with her scent, her taste, to know or care what was happening around him. When her orgasm hit it shuddered the entire chair, but her hand kept his head still, even when he bent lower and plunged his tongue into her slit.

"Oh, God!" Her thighs snapped shut, nearly cutting off his air, but he continued to drink from her. He reached underneath the folds of her skirt for her buttocks and slid his hands under the elastic waistband up her sides, holding her in place as she threatened to slide forward from the chair. He felt her entire body heave with the next orgasm, and for a second had to wonder how long it had been since somebody had done this to her.

Or if at all.

He finally lifted away, gazing at her weary, sated expression with his own sticky grin. He could not lean back too far, as the edge of the table blocked him from straightening. "Now," he gasped, "about those gorgeous tits of yours..."

Ellie obligingly moved her chair back so he could get up from underneath the table, and she tugged at his belt, then his fly. He took the opportunity to fondle her breasts, choking back a laugh as Ellie struggled to free his erection.

"Need help there, babe?"

Ellie gritted her teeth, her face reddening as her battle with the zipper turned comical. A quick flinch and she thrust the tip of her thumb between her teeth, as if catching it on a sharp piece of metal. "Couldn't you have sworn sweatpants?" she groaned. She was like a pouting teenager now, acting as if being told she might never have sex thanks to the mishaps of designer jeans. Brady released one breast and cupped her chin, tilting her face up to his.

"Hey now. Relax. C'mere." He bent forward and kissed her. She tasted of soy sauce and plums, an interesting combination with his "dessert." That stifled laugh finally came forward as she whimpered over his breaking away. "We got all night, babe, don't worry," he assured her, "even if I have to cut myself out of these jeans."

Ellie eyed his bulging crotch and smirked. "I have scissors," she offered. A tempting offer, but Brady was not sure he wanted a blade of any sort that close to him. He pulled his billfold from his back pocket and slapped it next to Ellie's plate. Then he kicked off his sneakers and worked the zipper himself until it came loose. He shrugged out of the jeans, then his briefs, and pulled off his T-shirt, discarding everything in the corner of the alcove with Ellie's blouse. Ellie wasted no time in adding her skirt to the pile, her awed gaze locked to his cock.

"Holy shit," she muttered, eyes saucer-wide, as she reached for him. "This is going to taste so good."

But Brady gently brushed her gaze away and reached for the billfold. *Yes!* There was one left.

"What?" Ellie asked, disappointed. "I can't have dessert?" She watched him roll on the condom and her expression softened. "I don't mind if you come in my mouth. I think I'd like that."

Brady said nothing, but helped her to stand. He would have enjoyed nothing better as well. "I'd like that," he said, turning her chair to face the mirror, "but if I don't get into your pussy right now I might just die."

Ellie sighed. "Well, we can't have that."

Brady sat in Ellie's chair, legs wide, his sheathed cock at full attention. Ellie moved to straddle him, but he had her face the mirror and bend forward, spreading her lips apart with his fingers before settling her gently on top of him. Ellie's breath caught in her throat as his cock impaled her pussy, and Brady brought her back against his chest, his hands tight around her waist.

He nudged his lips against her shoulder, kissing a trail to her neck. "Watch the mirror," he whispered gruffly in her ear, and she obeyed. Together they studied their reflections, the passion that connected them and the slow, grinding thrust of Brady's hips against Ellie's, arched forward so both could see her slick core moving up and down his cock.

"Watch," he echoed, and nudged her again when she tilted her head back and closed her eyes. "Watch. Look at you fucking me. God, is that beautiful or what?"

Ellie's eyes snapped open at the image before them, and she smiled. She brought her hands around his waist as his slid up her sides to knead her breasts. "I've never done anything like this before," she said. "I feel so…" She shook her head; the words would not come.

"Sexy? Wild?"

"I was going to say naughty," Ellie countered and craned her neck to briefly claim his mouth with hers. "I think I like being a naughty girl."

"I think I like you being naughty, too. I like

you, period." It was not a lie, either, he realized. This woman was incredible, and a fast learner where turning him on was concerned. Soon her hands covered his to coach him on where and how she liked to be touched, and once he was plucking her nipples on his own she brought one hand lower to finger her clit while he continued to thrust upward into her.

And when she contracted her pussy and squeezed his cock tightly, he felt the sensation rack his entire body. He had wanted this to last, but the feelings were as tortuous as they were pleasurable. This rhythm would have to be sped up if he wanted relief.

He coaxed her feet to the ground and bent her forward so that her hands braced against the mirror. Still inside her, he lifted himself from the chair, then grasped her hips, and thrust harder and faster into her. Her breasts wobbled underneath her, her head swung low from her shoulders, skin slapped against skin. Each deep stroke elicited from her a low moan, punctuated by a throaty laugh every time Brady swiveled his hips in one direction to alter the angle of entry into her pussy.

He looked down at their joined bodies, at his cock disappearing into that tight, moist warmth. Why had he let himself go for so long without this?

His gaze panned her bare back, to her thrashing shoulders and hair. It was definitely worth the wait, though. *She* was worth the wait.

When he finally came and let out his own deep

cry, Ellie matched him in volume, arching her face to the ceiling and pressing into him, tightening her channel until Brady's softening cock could no longer stay inside unaided. With one final thrust he slid out of her and onto the chair, exhausted, and drew Ellie onto his lap.

Arms wrapped around her, he nuzzled her left arm out of the way, leaned forward, and kissed the side of her breast. "Well," he panted, "I don't know about you, but I can't wait to see what we're having for breakfast."

NINE

Ellie wondered if they would make it to breakfast. Her nerves were so ignited, her skin so on fire, that she feared venturing into the kitchen to turn on the stove, lest her entire body combust upon proximity with the pilot light. What this man, now lying naked next to her in her bed, did to her was beyond orgasmic, regardless of his fame and fortune.

"Um, sweetheart, no," he moaned, and eased away as she pressed her bare backside against him. She had felt the stirring of another erection against her body and understood. Because of the stagnancy of her love life, Ellie had not bothered to keep any condoms in the apartment, nor had she anticipated that tonight's dinner would lead to the best sex of her life. Eventually in a week or so, if she were lucky, but not right afterward.

Brady had only the one they used, and Ellie doubted he would warm to the idea of seeing whether it could be resuscitated for future use.

It ached, though, to be so close to him and see his cock thickening with want. Exhausted as she was, she was far from being completely sated. She wanted that man's cock slamming inside her again until she could feel him in her chest. She wanted him inside her every way possible, fucking her mouth, her ass, and sliding his slick shaft between the valley of her breasts, until he was drained dry.

Damn, girl. What did this man do to her? Even at her horniest, she had never entertained such thoughts. Could it be his association with Claire, or the stories she had assumed were true about other rock singers that could be applied to him?

She could tell he wanted more, too, but this was not New York City. There were no 24-hour drugstores nearby to solve this dilemma. Even if there were, Ellie was sure she did not want either of them to leave this bed for one second. They were going to have to be creative in order to find release.

Ellie smiled at that thought.

"Turn over, then." She motioned to Brady and he sleepily complied, facing away from her on her side. This granted her a nice view of the ass that had so nicely filled his jeans. It looked even nicer *au naturel.*

"Good enough to eat," she purred. "Which reminds me, I was deprived of dessert." With that, she rose slightly to change position so that she lay facing his lower torso, her legs curled behind her, knees resting on her pillow. Brady rolled onto his back, his erection slowly returning.

"You're in luck," he said. "This is the last one."

Let's hope not. Ellie dipped a hand between his thighs and gently massaged his scrotum. She kissed a soft patch of skin near his thatch of pubic hair and rested her cheek there, staring up at him. What a gorgeous landscape. "This has to be the wildest thing I've ever done," she confessed.

Brady tilted his neck forward and peered down at her with a wide smile. "What, touching a man's balls? I can think of things you did earlier that could qualify as wilder than that."

"I meant having sex with a guy I just met," Ellie said, laughing.

Brady rested his head back again, supporting it with one hand. "Okay, then. I was starting to think maybe you really were a fast learner."

"I mean, I don't want you to get the idea that this is something I do all the time..."

"It's not?" Brady's expression registered mock surprise. "I thought this was the standard Dareville welcome, what with there hardly being anything on TV and no bars open past nine."

Ellie giggled. "No bars at all, it's a dry county, remember? Yeah, Dareville may be a sleepy little town, but it doesn't mean the natives are listless."

"The native are restless, I see. I think I'm going to like it here."

Ellie's eyes turned back to his cock; she wrapped her forefingers around the base and idly stroked his girth. She wanted to take him deep inside her mouth, but she liked talking with him, and said as much aloud. Tough choice.

"You should have learned ventriloquism, then," Brady joked.

"There's a skill every elementary teacher needs." Ellie rolled her eyes, and leaned over to quickly lick his shaft from bottom to top, swirling her tongue over the tip before planting a kiss there.

"Oh, that's nice," he moaned, and reciprocated by stroking her pussy, tracing the edge of her slit with his middle finger. Ellie felt her juices immediately surface.

"So what's the wildest thing you've ever done?" she asked, wondering what his answer would be. Considering his touring history, the parties he must have attended, and the starlets the tabloids claimed he had dated, she was certain he would mention something, even if he changed names and places.

Brady chuckled, suddenly coy. "Oh, you don't want to hear about any of that."

"Yes, I do," Ellie cajoled. "Come on. Living in the Big Apple, working for all those famous people, you *had* to have let your hair down once or twice."

"I don't know," Brady wheedled. He inserted his middle finger deep into her slit and stroked her from the inside in a come hither motion. Ellie stifled a breath. Was he looking for her G-spot? Did she even have one? Nobody had ever struck gold before. "This is pretty wild right here."

"Is this the first time you had sex with a woman you just met?" If he said yes, he had to be lying, Ellie decided. Surely Brady Garriston had partaken of a groupie or two back in the day. A girl in every town, or every other town, with maybe a few on the bus rides in between.

Brady half-shrugged. "Could be. Maybe not, I

can't say for sure. The seventies were a blur, and it got worse inside Studio 54 because of the fog machines."

"Come on, you must remember *some* things," Ellie said. "Okay, then, have you ever had two women at once?"

"Yeah. Just a few hours before I came here, in fact."

She looked at him, open-mouthed, and his face broke into a wide grin as he laughed.

Ellie's response was to slide her hand back down to his scrotum and squeeze until her fingers met. Brady let out a surprised howl, but thankfully did not appear annoyed.

"Hey, now," he said through a pained laugh. "You think that's wise to do while I got hold of you like this?" He massaged her vaginal wall even faster, causing Ellie's toes to curl. She felt no orgasmic sensations, but was soaked all the same. "I could stop, you know."

"I could stop, too," Ellie threatened, and released her own grip. Brady's hand stilled and the two stared at each other for several seconds until one of them spoke again.

It was Ellie. "You blinked."

"Damn it." Brady's wavered from side to side, then offered Ellie a complacent grin. "Truce?"

"Truce," Ellie agreed, and leaned forward again to take his cock into her mouth just as he urged her to move her hips on either side of his head so he could enjoy a second helping of dessert.

* * *

"What's with all the questions, anyway?" he asked, sounding somewhat uncomfortable. The sixty-nine had been amazing, his orgasm explosive, though the blood pounded through Brady's temples. He could have kept coming forever if possible, and no doubt Ellie would gladly have swallowed every last drop.

With that over, he was grateful for the opportunity to come up for air, and now he lay back on the bed, with Ellie snuggled into his side and fingering one of his nipples.

"Just want to know more about who you are, and what you like," Ellie said. "Something I probably should have done before I flashed you under my dining table."

"I'm not complaining about that," Brady chuckled, and exhaled as Ellie pinched a tender spot that sparked a pleasurable shock through his nervous system. "Oh, God, Cl—"

Her head shot up and she looked at him expectantly. Brady's mouth clamped shut. *Shit.* He was about to call her by Claire's name. Did she perceive that?

She smiled. "Did you say something? I wasn't paying attention."

Brady exhaled, happy to have dodged a bullet. "Closer, I said," he said, tightened his grip on Ellie's waist. "You can come a little closer."

"Any closer and I'll be underneath the mattress."

"How is it you're suddenly not paying attention, anyway?" Brady teased. "I thought you wanted to know all about me."

"I do, but my mind's beginning to wander. With a body like yours, you can't blame me, either. Besides, you're not very forthcoming, are you?" Ellie countered.

"I came more than once tonight, as I recall."

"Have you ever been with two women at once?" Ellie asked again.

Brady sighed. She was not going to let this go. Yes, he had enjoyed two women at once, more than once, and told her so, noting her poker face. "And, since you're probably going to ask anyway," he added, "I've also participated in an orgy, had sexual encounters with other men outside of that particular orgy, and at one time shared a woman with another man." The other man had been Cal, he remembered. One night many, many years ago. The woman's name, like many in his past, escaped him. "Senior year was the best."

He searched Ellie's face for a reaction, wondering if she would curl away in disgust. Claire, he recalled, had winced at his story of being arrested for indecent exposure during an eighties tour—he had been drunk and wandered away from a hotel pool with nothing but a beer bottle and a washcloth hanging from his erection. Smartly, he had elected to refrain from mentioning the saucier experiences of his life to her.

But Ellie rested her chin on his chest and peered at him through her lashes. "Define 'sexual encounters' with other men," she posed. "What, you sucked a man's cock, or took one up the old..." She frowned. "I can't think of a euphemism for anal sex. How about that?"

"Packing fudge? Driving in a pylon? Taking a trip up the old Hershey Highway?" Brady raised his eyebrows up and down. "Shall I go on?" Instead he laughed at Ellie's bewildered expression and continued, "Okay, okay. Receiving end of oral, giving end of anal, never vice versa. Satisfied?"

"Maybe." Ellie sounded coy. "The guy you had the three-way with, did you do him?"

"No." Even at his most inebriated, having sex with Cal had never crossed his mind. Not that he found the notion incestuous, it just never happened. "No, we mainly concentrated on her. That I do recall."

"Man, I'd love to have two men at once," Ellie sighed. "To feel two hard bodies pressing against me, inside me at the same time, kissing me all over…" She caressed his chest and kissed the nipple she had been plucking.

Hello. Brady blinked. Could this person actually be one of Claire's relatives? The two may look alike, but they were definitely polar opposites.

What was that he had thought about opposites attracting? Well, whoever had coined the phrase was clearly full of it.

"Interested?" he posed.

Ellie looked up at him. "You serious?"

"Yes. You like being the naughty girl, right?"

"*I love it.*"

"I like being naughty, too. And I like you being naughty, if it makes you happy," Brady said. "I'd like to help you stay naughty. I think that would make *me* happy."

"Well!" Ellie lifted slightly and rested against

him again. "I appreciate the offer, but I can't think of a man in Dareville I'd want to fuck, even solo. Present company excepted."

"Present company flattered." Brady hugged her close and lifted her head so he could nibble her ear. "So, if not a man, how about a three-way with another woman? You think you'd enjoy a soft, curvy body pressed up against yours? Doing this?" He slid one hand down from her breast and cupped her pussy.

"Maybe," she said, teasing. "Maybe I'd like doing the same to her, and sucking on her tits while you watch."

Brady's heart thrummed. "Would you eat her pussy while I watched?"

"If you were fucking me from behind."

Hello again. Definitely the black sheep of the family this woman was, he decided. Either that, or Claire was the lone sexual prude among a pack of horndogs. Ellie was completely sober now, and he could only imagine what ideas would come to her mind when drunk.

Whichever way, he was truly questioning the wisdom of using this woman to pursue the lovely lawyer. Claire was wonderful, yes, a vivacious woman and good in bed. Any man would be lucky to have her.

Ellie, however, was a category five hurricane, uprooting his heart and taking it on the ride of his life. He did not want it to end, either. His hand still on her mound, he slipped a finger between her folds and tapped at her clit.

"Oh, stop it," she whined and slapped him

away when his touch intensified. "You're overloading my senses. And I have to work in the morning. How am I supposed to teach a bunch of kids phonics while I'm thinking of you all day, and what you do to me?"

"Just think, don't speak anything incriminating, and you'll be fine." And Brady kissed her softly, running his tongue across her lips and gently prying apart her mouth. She tasted of him. They remained intertwined and kissing until she broke free and drifted into sleep.

Brady watched the smile play on her lips and wondered how her dreams compared to what they had experienced together. Was she reliving every moment they had shared, or conjuring up new and exciting play? Anything she had in mind for the future, he would definitely consider. Hell, he would just do it, no questions asked.

Words crowded his consciousness. Lyrics, rhymes, melody. He needed to write them down before they dissolved into memory, he knew. A song was conceived in the wake of their coupling. Ellie had awakened in him the passion and inspiration he had desperately sought in Europe, and thought he could find with Claire.

Claire. He could never be what Claire wanted him to be, he realized. She was partly right about him. He did not think himself immature, but he was wild, and he needed somebody on an even playing field. Ellie could be that person. She had not blinked when he talked of his same-sex encounters; Claire would have treated him like a leper. He had been wrong, too, *Ellie* was his muse.

His vibrant, sexy muse.

He frowned. There was, of course, the problem of Gary Stone. Ellie had made love with Gary Stone, not Brady Garriston. He was going to have to reveal himself sooner than he anticipated, he knew, and suddenly he dreaded the moment. As considerate as Ellie seemed to partaking of sexual adventures, it did not mean she would take so kindly to being deceived. Every innuendo, every loving endearment, could be easily forgotten if she decided she could not trust him, and told him to leave.

Brady swallowed. He would have to take the risk. He would break the news on their next date, he promised himself.

He watched her sleep, and pondered whether or not to gently pry himself away from her, dress, and leave. He wanted to get home and write down the lyrics brewing in his head. Ultimately, though, his fatigue won, and he closed his eyes, trusting his memory to preserve what Ellie had given him.

He was deep into sleep as Ellie snuggled against his chest and clutched his hip. "Oh, Brady," she whispered.

TEN

He saw her every night after that for three weeks straight. Some nights she entertained him at her apartment with homemade fare, and on others he played host at the cottage, accompanied by an impressive collection of jazz CDs and takeout pizza. The piano he had leased from a shop in Virginia Beach provided them some enjoyment as Brady obliged Ellie by showcasing his musical talent, but nothing he did with the keyboard was as pleasurable to her as the talents he displayed in bed. Brady estimated they alone were propping up the Dareville drugstore with his frequent purchases.

They made love standing in the shower, in the back seat of his car, and on the chaise lounge on her back patio, risking the full view of her neighbors. Using Brady's satellite television subscription, they watched adult films despite his distaste for them, because it was what Ellie wanted. Every time they did so, however, they rarely made it to the end of a movie without mimicking the onscreen action. Ellie had also liked their first coupling experience so much that Brady affixed mirrored tiles to the ceiling above his bed so she could watch every time they were at his place.

The sex, while frequent, only made for part

of his growing attraction to her. They talked in earnest about everything—politics, art, and music—and with each passing day Brady realized how many common interests they shared. They both liked to hike, favored the Mets, and shared an appreciation for good food.

Being with Ellie also took years off his life; the difference was evident every time he looked in the mirror. He appeared less haggard, his gray eyes alive with color. They were like teenagers exploring each other's bodies and desires, oblivious to the world around them, indifferent to any dire consequences.

The only thing Brady had not done, though, was to tell her the truth. Every time a moment would grow serious between them and he would open his mouth to speak, Ellie would either kiss him or press him into service again. The thought to reveal his true self would be forgotten in the haze of another earth-shattering orgasm.

Another thing he liked about Ellie, too, was her bluntness. Whatever she wanted, she didn't ask for with vague hints. Three weeks after their first dinner, they were at his cottage, finishing an *actual* dessert of pound cake and strawberries when Ellie asked him point blank to "fuck her tits."

Brady choked on his last bite; strawberry juice squirted and trickled down his chin. "Now?"

Ellie propped an elbow on the dining table and rested her chin in the palm of her hand. From her pocket she produced a small bottle of K-Y. "When you're finished eating. You'll need your strength."

Mercy. "You carry that stuff around with you now?"

"They always taught us in Scouts to be prepared."

"I think I'll refrain from making any further comments," Brady said warily.

Ellie smiled. "Smart man."

Before long they were both naked, and Brady was straddling her on the living room carpet. Ellie cupped her breasts and compressed them together while Brady rammed his unsheathed, lubricated cock in the tightened space. The friction of her skin against his sent pleasured reverberations throughout his body, but nothing caused his heart to soar as high as that look of ecstasy in those beautiful green eyes.

"Nobody's ever done this to me before," she confessed, breathless.

"I find that hard to believe, unless I'm the first person you asked." Ellie had been as frank about her sexual history with him as he was with her, though her fantasies far outweighed actual experience.

"You're not, just the first to oblige." Ellie pouted. "I've never met a man as sexually creative as you."

He felt a twinge of satisfaction at the compliment, and with being her first at something.

Brady sat up slightly but had to brace his palms against the carpet to keep from losing balance. The tip of his shaft, glistening with precum, poked through the top of her breasts and Ellie arched her neck forward. She caught the pearly drop with the tip of her tongue, eliciting from him an anguished cry. The condoms were in the bedroom, how was he going to get there and back with one without either coming *en route* or collapsing in pain?

Ellie's next words, though, solved that dilemma. "I want you to come on my tits," she said. "I want to rub you into my skin."

Brady looked at her, bemused, and continued to pump against her, so roughly that her entire body rubbed back and forth against the Berber carpet. Her language had become rather salty of late. Was this a new development he influenced?

He did not, though, get to ponder that very long, for the buildup in his scrotum was too much to bear, and he jerked his cock out of that fleshy prison to come. With one hand cuffed around his shaft, he milked himself through a screaming orgasm. Hot come sprayed Ellie's breasts and she rubbed it into her skin, then licked the sticky substance from her fingers as Brady collapsed to one side.

"Mmm," came a throaty purr, tickling one ear. Ellie rolled onto his heaving chest, their bodies becoming glued, and kissed him square on the lips. "Thank you, sweetie. That's one more thing I can cross off my list."

Brady took her buttocks in hand and gently rubbed the embedded rug marks. At this point if Ellie had asked him to next rob the Dareville Bank he would have sprang from the floor to find a ski mask. "How long is this list, exactly?" he asked.

They had yet to fulfill some of the racier things Ellie wanted to do, like threesomes and public sex, and Brady respected her discretion in these matters. She was a schoolteacher, and known around Dareville. Some parents and school administrators would not take kindly to hearing of an elementary teacher's sexual exploits.

Assuming he got around to telling her that he was really Brady Garriston, and assuming she would not have a problem with it, Brady decided he would have to get her to New York in order to make her dreams reality. He knew Cal would be up for some fun, at least.

"It's not that long, but I do keep adding things as we go along," she replied.

Brady gently set her to one side and eased himself from the carpet. "Well, hopefully the next item can wait a bit. I feel a song coming on." With that, he took to the piano bench and launched immediately into a jazzy instrumental. In a way, his playing was nothing short of orgasmic as well for him. The music seemed to flow through his body, out his fingers and onto the keys. The sensation gave him great pleasure, and that Ellie could inspire this music so quickly intensified the feeling.

He didn't hear Ellie get up and retreat to the bedroom. Minutes later she was standing behind him with a condom clamped between two fingers. She crushed her breasts against his bare, rippling back as she caressed his shoulders and neck.

"You know, I can think of other ways to expend that energy." Her breath tickled his ear as his fingers danced maniacally across the keys.

Mercy. "Baby, I'm still spinning. You'll have to give me a few minutes at least," Brady said, his expression glowing with want.

"Okay, but just a few," she conceded, but Brady could detect a hint of jest in her voice.

Ellie paused to listen. "This is great. Is it Gershwin?"

"Actually, it's Ga—" His voice faltered, but the music did not. The piece was original Garriston, composed in the afterglow of their recent lovemaking. In fact, he wondered if he shouldn't be writing some of it down before he forgot half of it. The thought was tempting, but he wondered, too, if he revealed that he wrote music would Ellie figure out who he really was.

His fingers slowed, the notes faded into silence. Was this the right time to reveal his true self, to bare his soul to match his bare body? He craned his neck to look at Ellie, but her question seemed to be forgotten as she found new a distraction in kissing the back of his neck.

She pressed her hands into the bench on either side of him and traced the top of his spine with her tongue. The touch sent chills through him, and he exhaled slowly. "Am I disrupting your playing?" she asked.

"You damn well know the answer to that," he said, his voice low. Inwardly, however, he groaned. He was still Gary Stone, for at least another day.

She lifted her head and kissed his cheek. "How about a piano lesson, then? I've never played before, but you seem to think I'm a fast learner."

"I won't argue." Brady ushered Ellie out of the way to inch back the bench to give her room. "But you'll want to be centered at the keyboard, so it looks like you'll have to sit on my lap."

He watched Ellie eye his cock with amusement. Limp against his abdomen, it struggled nonetheless to show signs of life. "If you weren't going to suggest it, I was," she giggled, and Brady arranged himself comfortably before settling Ellie's luscious bottom on his thighs.

Ellie set the condom on the bench next to them. Brady tilted her to one side and grabbed both her hands, positioning her fingers on various white keys. As she squirmed for comfort, no doubt intentionally, his cock jerked and twitched between them. "Why don't we start with something simple, like Chopsticks?" he suggested, and guided her hands to depress the necessary keys, pounding out the basic piano exercise.

"This doesn't sound like Chopsticks." Ellie grimaced.

"That's because we're playing too slow. And you're hitting the wrong keys. No, this one." He laughed as Ellie wrested from his grip and plucked keys at random, messing up his rhythm as he tried to play the song normally.

The rhythm between their bodies, however, played much more smoothly. Ellie relaxed against him and swiveled her lower body from left to right, triggering his arousal until she gave up on fingering the keyboard altogether and moved to the pianist.

"I'm not big on chopsticks, anyway," she said

a baby voice, and stroked his bare thighs. "I prefer something more substantial. Something *thicker*, like that nice instrument poking me in the back right now."

Brady responded by lifting his hands from the keyboard and cupping her still sticky breasts. He trailed kisses across her back. "You're right, perhaps this isn't the proper time for a lesson. Too many distractions."

"How long did it take you to go from Chopsticks to Gershwin?"

"A number of years, but I doubt I'd have gotten far with a gorgeous, naked lady on my lap while I was practicing."

Ellie giggled, and parted her legs slightly. She then moved one of his hands down to her pussy. Brady got the message and burrowed through her folds to stroke her clit. "Yes," she sighed, "I think your hands are much better suited to this."

"I do enjoy these private performances," Brady murmured into her shoulder, and quickened his pace. It didn't take long for Ellie to climax, her cries punctuated by several miscues at the piano as her hands hit keys at random.

"Well," Brady said as she her body rocked against his slowly, "I think you hit the middle C there."

"I'd rather you hit the G."

Brady shifted her in place. His cock was certainly hard enough now to accomplish that. He reached for the condom and eased her to stand as he quickly rolled it on. But as he widened his legs and parted her pussy lips for contact, she stilled him with one word.

"No."

"You want to move to the bedroom?"

Ellie shook her head. Her face was only partly visible, but he could see she was biting her lip.

"It's not that." She paused. "I want you inside me...the other way."

Brady raised an eyebrow. Why the sudden demureness in speech from the woman who earlier said, "Fuck my tits"?

"You want me to fuck your ass?"

She nodded. "I've never done that before either. I think the time is right."

Brady felt his blood surge. This was certainly a day for firsts.

He pointed to the bottle of lubricant, still on the carpet. "We'll need some of that," he said, and Ellie darted quickly away to retrieve the bottle, which she handed to Brady. Brady scooted the bench back further, squeezed a dime-size drop of the clear gel onto his fingers, and had Ellie position herself in a half bend using the top of the piano for support.

"You let me know if it hurts, and we'll stop," he said, and teased her anus with one greased finger. Ellie gasped at the new sensation, and Brady felt her muscles tighten around him. Oh, his cock was going to feel so good inside her like this.

He dared a second finger, moving them gently in and out of her. Ellie's breathing hitched slightly, and he thought he detected a pained whimper. "That hurt?"

"No," she wheezed. "Please, let me feel your

cock inside me."

"Careful now." He positioned his shaft at her anal opening and had her sit slowly. He wished he could've seen the range of emotions flit across her face—shock to pleasure to excitement—but with her facing away from him it was impossible. He had only the rapid beating of her heart as a gauge, and he could feel it vibrate her entire body.

When he was snug inside her, he guided her body up and down his shaft, slowly at first. The random tightening of her muscles caused his lower body to quiver. "How's that feel?" he whispered.

"S'nice."

"It won't hurt as much next time."

"Good." She licked her lips, and his heartbeat matched hers. There was going to be a next time.

She pried his hands from her waist and settled them on the piano, then braced against his thighs to control her movements. "Play something," she said.

He brushed the keys. Disjointed butterfly noises quietly erupted. He didn't quite know what to say, or do. Playing piano while engaged in intercourse was a first for *him*. "Any requests?"

"Something slow," she groaned, "and sexy."

"Whatever the lady wants." He brushed aside her feet with his own so he could better control the pedals and began a slow, deep Beethoven sonata which suited their rhythm. Each note of the familiar tune pounded in his ears, barely masking Ellie's ecstatic groans as she continued to grind into him. Each downward stroke caused him to hit the keys a bit harder, until he thought his fingers would callus from the impact. Occasionally he would miscue following a jerked movement from her, but he kept the song even with their pace, which quickened as the music's tempo did.

No matter how hard he hit the keyboard, or how loud the notes produced from the piano, though, the music pitched low from Ellie's throat seemed to overpower it. But as Brady leaned over to see Ellie's lips clamped shut in a dreamy smile, he realized the noise was coming from him.

She squeezed again; his cock felt trapped in a pleasurable vice. He had wanted to last longer for her, but found he couldn't. He came with a guttural cry, and simultaneously ended the sonata abruptly as his fingers splayed the keyboard in a final orgasmic note.

He grasped her waist with one hand while the other braced the piano to keep them from falling off the bench. They were both drenched with sweat and gasping. His heart pounded so fast and so far from his chest it felt as if it had burst through him into Ellie.

"You," Ellie said, craning her neck back to attempt a kiss on his lips, "are my favorite musician."

Brady managed a grin. "You thought that was good, just wait until the encore."

ELEVEN

The charade had gone long enough, he decided after last night's incredible recital. Ellie had to know the truth, and she would know when she came over after school let out.

When Ellie worked, Brady was very productive at the piano. During their time together, he had composed nearly enough material for a new album. Lined music sheets littered his dining table, and spiral notebooks filled with ink rested on his kitchen counter. Six new songs, sensual and vibrant, echoed in his head as he imagined Cal's bass accompaniment along with the proper percussion and guitar notes. He had to get to a studio soon and get this album recorded and mixed. Get the tapes to his label, get the finished product in stores.

Tell Ellie the truth, pray that she would not be mad. Get her to quit her job and join him on tour to support the album. They could make love in every state in the Union, backstage at the Grammys, anywhere and everywhere she wanted.

He looked up from a recent stack of notes and checked the microwave clock. School was almost out for the day, but he knew not to call for another forty minutes or so, as Ellie usually had to finish up a few chores around her classroom.

Sometimes, too, a colleague would ensnare her in small talk before she could escape. Almost always, it was that Lauren woman Ellie often mentioned, come to Ellie's classroom to moon over some local widower who did not know the divorcee existed. It definitely sounded like Miss Lauren could use what Ellie was getting.

Brady smiled to himself. Strange, though, that Ellie had never suggested that Lauren be invited to join in their play. Other things about Lauren that Ellie had confided told him that perhaps Lauren would be a willing party to their mischief. Perhaps Ellie thought it too awkward to involve a co-worker, he decided.

He looked at the clock again. His groin tingled. Eight hours without Ellie, while musically productive, had been torture, and he could not wait another hour to be with her.

He rose from the table with some music sheets, grabbed his keys from the kitchen counter, and headed out the door. Ellie's school was not far; he would surprise her after the final bell, and perhaps earn some much-needed detention.

And when he told her the truth, he hoped she would not expel him from her life.

* * *

"Miss Shaw?"

Ellie sat hunched over her desk, doodling her initials and Brady's in a pencil-drawn heart on the calendar blotter.

"Miss Shaw?" the young girl standing next to her persisted. Ellie looked up at her with a dreamy smile, then remembered where she was. *Wake up, woman*, she admonished herself. There were only a few minutes left in the school day, and though her class was behaving reasonably well, she still had to pay attention to them.

Fantasies about Brady, like the XXX-rated one she had been harboring when her student interrupted, could wait.

"I'm sorry, Judy, did you want something?" Ellie asked.

The young girl held aloft two chalkboard erasers, coated with white dust, and Ellie needed to hear no further questions. The end of each school day always brought at least one student eager to perform such extracurricular tasks. Ellie laughed and gently guided the girl back to the chalkboard to replace the erasers on their ridged rest.

"That's okay, sweetheart, I think they'll keep another day. You can clap them out tomorrow. Why don't go ahead and pack up to go home?"

Judy nodded and retreated to her desk, and Ellie watched as she and her other students shuffled papers into homework folders and put away pencils. She had such a good class this year, in terms of behavior and scholarship; she loved "her kids" dearly, and as a whole they appeared to love being at DPA. She loved this job.

Of course, other thoughts than work occupied her lately. Ellie smiled again, thinking of Brady, and last night. Her heart swelled. Could she be falling for him as well?

The shrill peal of the final bell tore through these thoughts, and her students rose as one, awaiting her signal.

Ellie shook away the cobwebs and clapped her hands. "Okay, everybody, great day today. Let's get you home."

A pang seized her heart as she gently rose from her desk to line up the class for dismissal. It seemed as the school year progressed, she found herself wondering if each day might be the last time she would be able to teach these children. To hear Lauren talk, the building committee was getting nowhere, and the state inspector was tapping his watch. No way would the children be permitted to remain in a building that the state believed could collapse on them at any time. Something had to be done.

Her gait was stiff as she escorted her class past other uniform lines of younger and older students to the school's main entrance, where a fleet of buses and minivans awaited to ferry each child home. Ellie tugged at her buttoned collar. Children, parents, and teachers saw only Miss Ellie Shaw dressed primly in a dark floral blouse and beige pencil skirt. Underneath, though, her body was swathed in a see-through black lace catsuit with a plunging neckline and a split crotch for easy access. Ellie had purchased it express delivery from an Internet lingerie catalog, and hoped to drive directly to Brady's after work and surprise him with a slow, sensuous striptease. Proper schoolmarm turns vixen.

But the suit itched like crazy, all over. Ellie had spent the entire day at work resisting the urge to tear at her clothes and scratch her skin raw. *Oh, well*, she thought with a sigh. Maybe she could slip it off in the ladies' faculty lounge and use it to tie him to the bed instead. Afterward he could slather her in calamine lotion.

When the last of her students waved goodbye before climbing into a station wagon, Ellie dashed back to her room to gather her things. She wanted to get out as soon as possible. She wanted to dodge any last minute requests from the administration and definitely any whining from Lauren. She was officially off the clock, and wanted to be on top of Brady.

As she stuffed spelling tests into her briefcase, though, her movements slowed. Tonight, too, she knew she was going to have to say something to Brady. The past three weeks for her had been incredible, with last night being what she hoped would be the first of many apexes. Never before had she felt so alive, so desired, so pleasured. Yet, she felt guilty for experiencing it when Brady believed she thought he was somebody else.

She wondered, too, why Brady had allowed so much time to lapse without saying anything. Did he think she would have treated him differently, or did he suspect she was some kind of gold digger, and maybe try to get pregnant and pressure him in some way?

She had no intentions of doing either. She loved kids, but was hardly ready for one of her own, much less one sired by a famous man.

Her heart numbed. Maybe using the assumed name would allow him to cut out of town easier, make it more difficult for her to track him down later? Claire had been adamant about his flighty behavior, so perhaps this was a ploy he used with other women in the past?

She shook her head. *No, no, no.* She promised herself that she was not going to read too much into this relationship. She accepted it for what it was; she wanted to have fun, and Brady obliged her without reservation. Eventually he was going to go back to New York, or wherever, and resume his career as the great Brady Garriston. They had made no commitments, so whether he chose to move forward with or without her, or bother to reveal his true self, would be a decision with which she had to live.

So long as he obliged her one more thing, she reminded herself with a wicked smile, thinking of the rolled-up paper sack in her car—a secret purchase from an adult novelty store in Virginia Beach that she planned to bring over tonight. If this wild ride were to suddenly end, and she forced off the carousel, she wanted one permanent reminder of the most intense, amorous time of her life.

A light tap on the door startled her, and Ellie whirled around to see those two dark eyes that instantly set her heart to throb staring at her with amusement. Brady leaned against the open doorway with his arms folded and hips thrust forward in a manner that enhanced the obvious bulge in his jeans.

"You were talking to yourself," he accused. "Is working with kids *that* stressful?"

"I was?" Ellie felt suddenly self-conscious. Her hand touched her throat; the black lace covering her skin seemed more binding than ever. What had she said? Moreover, how much had he heard?

If Brady suspected anything amiss, his expression said nothing to her. He sauntered into the classroom and grazed his thigh against the corner of her desk. "I hope you don't mind my coming over here," he said. "I thought I'd surprise you."

"You certainly did that," Ellie said, and hoped she had not sounded put off. She really was happy to see him, and just that flash of chest hair and skin exposed through the unbuttoned collar of his Oxford shirt set her hormones raging. She wanted to rush past him and lock the door, wipe away all of the evidence of the day's work on her desk, and fuck him on the hardwood top. If only she had some poster board to tape over the window in the door, in case a teacher or Mr. Yost walked past.

She shrugged to herself. So what if they did? Let them watch. That would satisfy another fantasy Brady would likely help her fulfill.

Brady leaned forward and smiled. "You're doing it again," he sang.

Ellie blushed. "Sorry. I guess I'm prone to thinking out loud, especially when you're around to scramble my brains."

"That so?" Brady rested his hip on the desk corner. "Well, rest assured it's something I'd never do intentionally. I like your brains the way they are."

"Why, thank you, kind sir." Ellie mock bowed.

"And your tits." Brady licked his lips. "Which I could suck on for days."

Ellie cast a glance at the open door. The hallways were barren, far as she could see.

"Keep going."

"And your ass, which I want to dig my fingers into while I'm slamming hard inside you."

Ellie moved closer, exaggerating her steps to wiggle said ass for his benefit. The catsuit chafed her, but it was worth it to see the lust flare in Brady's eyes.

"And that sweet little pussy that just melts in my mouth," he finished, his voice husky.

"Young man," she scolded quietly, and draped one arm over his shoulder, "if you think that kind of talk is going to make you teacher's pet—"

"I'd rather pet the teacher." Brady cupped one breast and massaged.

"I think what you need is a good paddling," Ellie giggled. Their lips were close enough to touch now. "Or detention."

"How many more educational euphemisms do we need to go through before I can take you right here?" Brady's other hand slid down her back, around her hip, and slipped under the hem of her skirt, working its way back up again.

Ellie's answer was interrupted by a heavy sigh at her door, then a woman's voice calling her name. She jumped immediately away from Brady's touch to see Lauren entering the room.

"El, I'm so glad I caught you before you lef—oh!" Lauren skidded to a halt just behind Brady. "I'm sorry," she rejoined quickly. "I didn't realize you had—"

When Brady turned around to greet the teacher, Lauren's voice faded as Ellie's anxiety hit the ceiling. The memory of that day at Jake's, when Ellie first saw "Gary Stone" loping toward her, resurfaced in full color as Lauren's squeals bounced off the construction paper-covered walls.

Lauren did not see Gary Stone before her, she saw Brady Garriston. Brady Garriston the rock star, whom everybody thought was still dating her cousin, whom Ellie had agreed to ask to perform a benefit for the school.

Of course, she had forgotten agreeing to do that until this moment. She had been so preoccupied with the sex.

Lauren, however, had not. She took bewildered Brady's hand in hers and shook it vigorously, using her whole body, she appeared that nervous. "Oh, my God!" she exclaimed. "I don't fucking believe it. It's really you." She leaned over to better see Ellie over Brady's shoulder. "I mean, when Jake said…and you were all, like…"

"Lauren." Ellie tried to step in between them, but her colleague had such a tight grip on Brady's hand. Ellie could see his knuckles turning white, though his bemused expression remained unchanged. Of course, he was probably accustomed to woman fawning over him like this.

She had to say something, though, before Lauren spilled. "Lauren," she echoed, her hand on the flesh knot clamped around Brady's wrist. "This is not—"

"Mr. Garriston, I am a *huge* fan of your music," Lauren babbled as Brady's head bobbed. "When I found out that Ellie knew you through her cousin Claire, I thought it would be a long shot to get you to come down here—"

Ellie's head drooped and she eased away. *Fuck.* He would have to know now that she had been onto him the whole time. He would humor Lauren for show, find an excuse to break their date, and be on the first plane to New York without so much as a goodbye.

"—but I do take this to mean that you have agreed to Ellie's proposal?" Lauren cast a hopeful glance at her. Brady's gaze followed, then turned back to Lauren.

"Miss?" Brady began.

Lauren tittered. "Sorry. Lauren McKenna. I teach third grade, and I'm on the DPA Building Committee."

"Miss McKenna, a pleasure." Brady deftly pried her grip away with his free hand. "You'll have to forgive me when I ask that you be more specific. You see," he glanced at Ellie again, "Ellie has proposed quite a bit to me recently."

Ellie flushed deep red and hope Lauren did not notice.

"Oh." Lauren's voice rang with surprise. "Well, this would be the benefit concert idea we had, raising money for the building repair fund. We're rather short on benefactors and fundraising has been a bear, and when we found out about Ellie's connection to you, we thought it might be a good idea. I mean, your music is very popular here. No doubt a show would be a sellout."

Ellie rolled her eyes. How did Lauren know that for sure? "Lauren," she tried again. "This really isn't—"

"Is Claire here?" Lauren asked Ellie. "I haven't seen her in ages."

Brady straightened, and Ellie detected a grim line creasing his brow. *Uh-oh.* Here was where he was going to turn down Lauren and make his escape. She studied his face, as if for the last time, creating an indelible imprint in her memory.

"Actually, Claire and I are no longer seeing each other," Brady said quietly. "We sort of came to the mutual decision that we weren't suited for each other."

Lauren's face fell. "Oh, I'm sorry to hear that."

Brady nodded off the condolence. "Regardless of my personal relationships, though, I do sympathize with yours and Ellie's plight. That's why I made the trip down here from New York." He shoved his hands in his pockets and looked around the room. "I was just telling Ellie that I went to private schools, too. Seeing a school like this brings back some memories."

Ellie choked back a laugh and wondered how memories of grade school related to what they were really talking about when Lauren interrupted them.

Lauren's eyes widened. "I hope this means what I think it means," she said, giddy. "You're going to agree to do a benefit?"

"I'd be happy to," Brady said, then quickly braced against Ellie's desk with one hand as Lauren whooped for joy and grabbed him by the shoulders.

"Oh, God, you guys! This is great news!" she

cried. "We are going to make *so* much money doing this! We'll be able to rebuild DPA twice over."

Ellie, meanwhile, could only watch this scene unfold, powerless to move. What would possess him to accept this proposal? Did he feel obliged to do something to make up for the fact that his cover might have been blown? Why would he feel the need to do so? He could easily have said no, that his schedule would not allow it, and have been on his way.

Or, he could have simply tried the Gary Stone line on Lauren. It might have worked; it did on her once. What was he trying to prove here?

Lauren's continued babble broke into these thoughts, as her colleague grilled Brady for specific information—an agent to contact, phone numbers, an invitation to tonight's committee meeting.

Which he would probably blow off as he blew off Dareville entirely for the Norfolk airport.

But Brady surprised her again. "If you don't mind," he said, "I would prefer to work through Ellie. I don't have representation anymore, I handle my own business affairs, and I am trying to keep a low profile around here. Any information you have for me can be passed through her, and vice versa."

Lauren nodded vigorously. "Of course, I understand. You don't need fans beating down your door at all hours." She hitched her sliding purse strap over her shoulder and backed toward the door. "I'll tell the committee it's all set then, and maybe tomorrow we could meet for dinner and work over specifics, like a venue and tickets?"

"Sounds great. Make arrangements with Ellie tomorrow." Brady turned back to her, expecting Ellie to agree to act as mediator.

"Hm?" It seemed to her like the first time either of them realized she was still in the room. "Oh, yeah. Lauren, get with me at lunch tomorrow."

Lauren's farewell was an exaggerated fist pump as she floated happily out of the classroom. Ellie did not wait for her colleague's footsteps to echo down the hall into silence as she moved forward to quietly lock the classroom door.

She took a deep breath, then turned around to face Brady, to face those beautiful piercing eyes watching her no differently than they had in the past.

They called each other by name in unison, with Ellie using "Gary." There came an awkward pause, but Brady jumped in first with, "I have something to tell you."

Ellie's heart pounded. Would it be pointless to try to convince Brady that she still thought he was Gary Stone, now pretending to be Brady Garriston? *Of course it would, stupid.* He had seen the picture of Claire in her apartment. He knew she knew Claire, and that Lauren did, too.

"I have something to say, too," she said.

And they spoke in unison again.

"I really am Brady Garriston."

"I knew all along you're really Brady—"

They stopped in unison, too. Brady's expression was one of surprise, but not anger. It appeared, also, that he was surprised she seemed to be taking his news well.

"You know?" Brady asked. "Or rather, you knew before this?"

Ellie bit her lip and nodded. "At dinner, that first night. You saw the picture of me with Claire. I talk to her all the time, and I knew you'd gone out with her, and you said her name out loud. I heard you."

Brady swallowed, hard. "And you're not mad at me for being dishonest?"

"Not really. I was shocked at first, but I figured you had your reasons for wanting anonymity." Ellie traced a floor tile with the toe of her pump. "I don't think I would have offered you dessert if I was mad."

"Why *did* you offer me dessert? Some kind of revenge thing with Claire?"

"No." Ellie was shocked. "Claire's practically my sister. I've always lived vicariously through her, too, since she's so pretty and successful. I guess," she paused. "I guess just for once I wanted to know what it was like to *be* her, and to have something she had."

"Trust me. You are not Claire," Brady said softly. "And I wouldn't want it any other way."

"Gary," she chided, then huffed. "I mean—"

"I know what you mean, but I guess you can call me Brady now. Or Gary, I don't really mind," he said. "In fact, I kind of like you calling me that, especially in the heat of passion."

"Well, maybe that can be the teacher's name for her pet," she countered, smirking. Then, serious, she asked, "Are you mad at me?"

Brady frowned. "Why would I be mad at you? You've done nothing wrong."

"No, I knew about you from the start and said nothing. I could have called you out that first night, and instead I let things go three weeks without saying anything because I was enjoying myself so much. I didn't want it, us, to end just yet."

"You think I *wasn't* enjoying myself? You think I want this to end?" Brady's voice raised an octave, though he still did not sound angry to Ellie. He leaned back against the desk again and held out his arms. "Come here."

But Ellie was hesitant. There was one more thing she had to know first. "Did *you* come here to use me to get back at Claire?"

His arms fell to his sides and he sighed. Ellie's heart sank again. *Uh-oh.*

"The truth is that I had no idea you were Claire's cousin when we met. She never mentioned Dareville once, I happened to find this place on a map by random. Yes, I noticed you look a lot like her, and maybe that's what attracted me to you in the first place," he said. "Then I saw that picture on your shelf and nearly freaked. I mean, what were the odds of that?"

"I should have as much luck with the lottery," Ellie said, wistful. She took a tentative step closer, arms folded, though she really did want to leap right onto Brady and push him back against the desk top.

"The thought *had* crossed my mind that maybe if I eventually revealed myself to you, and behaved myself, maybe you would put in a good word for me to Claire," he continued, then added quickly, "Then we had dinner, and dessert..."

"Claire never offered you dessert?" Ellie asked coyly. "I heard different."

"Not like that." Brady's smile cut deep into her heart. "Nothing Claire is or has done compares to you, Ellie. Yes, Claire and I dated, and made love, and I thought at one time I could love her..."

Ellie stilled her legs, but the rest of her seemed to ethereally surge forward. She shivered, sensing the other shoe to drop in her favor.

"But you do so much more for me, Ellie. It's true what I told your friend a while ago. She and I weren't suited for each other, and I guess I couldn't see that for a while." His eyes reflected a sensuous honesty that touched her soul. Coupled with that voice, it was too much for Ellie to take. It took all of her willpower not to collapse into a puddle at his feet.

"The more I think about it, Claire was right. She's cautious where I'm reckless, and practical where I'm spontaneous. She needs a lover suitable to her needs, and I need you," Brady said. "And it's not just for the sex, either, which has been mind-blowing, to say the least." He reached into his back pocket and unfolded some papers. "Since I met you I started writing songs again. You know how long it's been since I've done that?"

Ellie did not know. "I know it's been a while since you had an album out," she said. "And I don't really know how you guys operate in that respect. I always thought some singers kept an arsenal of songs and recordings that don't make it to albums."

"Some do, but I've never been like that. Everything I've written has been recorded and released somewhere. There aren't going to be any lost Brady Garriston tapes coming out anytime soon." He smiled and tapped the papers in the heel of his hand. "But there's going to be an album of new material, thanks to you."

He offered her one sheet, which she took with a trembling hand. It was lined sheet music, with numerous penciled musical notes jotted across the rows of scales. Above all that was one short sentence: *"Ellie": words and music by Brady Garriston.*

"You wrote a song about me?" Ellie scanned the lyrics underneath each note. Not just any song, she realized, but a rather sexy one. Many of the endearments were familiar, things they had whispered to each other in bed. Ellie felt herself getting wet between her thighs just thinking about their pillow talk set to music. His music, his fingers expertly caressing piano keys the way he had set her skin to tingle.

"About you, for you. I'm dedicating the whole album to you, Ellie." Brady drew her closer; she did not resist, but let herself be enveloped as he pressed one hand against her head and kissed her cheek. The sheet music crumpled between them. "There wouldn't be an album without you. I'm going to rent out that studio in Virginia Beach and get right to work on it, in between rehearsals for this concert I've apparently committed to doing, of course."

"Why did you agree to that?" Ellie was still baffled. "You didn't have to let Lauren pressure you. You could have made up some excuse."

Brady nuzzled her neck. "Saving this school would make you happy, right?"

"Of course it would. This is a great school."

"Making you happy makes me happy, Ellie." Brady cupped a hand under her chin and pulled her face upward for a searing kiss. Ellie's entire body softened against his, and the discomfort of her undergarment was soon an afterthought.

When they finally broke away, Ellie asked, "Can I come to the studio and watch you in action? I'd love to be there when you record my song."

Brady chuckled. "If I said yes, I don't think the song would get recorded. I want to have you right there in the booth."

"In front of all those studio musicians and record producers?" Ellie giggled.

"With the tapes running."

"Now there would be an interesting recording," Ellie murmured. "But you'll sing it at the show?"

Brady kissed a trail from her lips down her neck, unbuttoning her blouse as he went. "Oh, I don't know sweetheart. There's still some work I want to do on it, and I want it to be perfect when I sing it live."

Ellie pouted.

"But," he conceded, "I'll sing it just for you. Anytime you want."

"I'd like that."

Ellie helped him pull back her blouse, revealing the top of the catsuit, which immediately elicited Brady's approval. His tongue slid down the bare flesh exposed in the low neckline, then cut a sharp left to tease one nipple.

"Brady," she moaned. She reached behind her to clear away some space on her desk. Like hell was she going to wait until they got home; she wanted his cock inside her now, and if anybody happened to catch a glimpse of Brady's bare ass as he pumped into her, so what? She was helping to save the school, and that person's job! She was owed at least this.

Brady took the nipple between his teeth and bit gently. Ellie hated to break contact, but she needed to do so in order to sit more comfortably on the desktop. She eased her ass further onto the hard wood, pushing aside pencils and papers, and hiked up her skirt to reveal the split crotch of her catsuit, which barely covered her slick pussy.

Brady positioned himself between her widening knees and smiled. "I like the new dress code," he said, and plunged one finger deep inside her.

Ellie arched her back, relishing the sensation as Brady's finger twirled inside her core. "Not as much as I like giving out assignments," she said, and looked up at him. "Speaking of which—"

"Yes, ma'am," Brady said, and lowered his face into her crotch. "Always willing to earn extra credit."

TWELVE

For once in the existence of the DPA Building Committee, solid decisions were made. It was decided that Brady's benefit concert would be held outdoors at Dareville Veteran's Memorial Park, since the town had no performing arts center or other such suitable venue large enough to accommodate a large audience. It did not make sense, it was reasoned, to have the show in Virginia Beach since the school was the reason for the show. A show date—two months from the day Brady met Lauren—and a rain date were scheduled to Brady's satisfaction, and he immediately set to work rehearsing his hit songs and the new material when he was not at the recording studio, laying down tracks for the album.

Through trustworthy contacts he found two excellent local musicians, a drummer and guitar player, for the album, and both were willing to play the live show for free. The publicity alone they would receive for the gig was worth the time invested, and Brady was equally blessed by the fact that he got along well with them.

His bassist, though, had to be Cal. He would not work with anyone else, and it took some conniving and cajoling to get his best friend to make the trip to "the sticks."

"Next thing you know you'll be straining to be heard over the hog calling contest at some Kentucky hillbilly fair," Cal had grumbled over the phone when Brady called him about the show.

"I promise you," Brady said on his end, watching a nude Ellie float through his master bedroom, preparing for bed, "it'll be worth your time."

Cal had continued to grumble upon arrival, down the airport terminal, and on the long, boring drive to Dareville. But when Cal met Ellie at the cottage, Brady had to laugh at his best friend's sudden change of heart. That night at dinner, Cal turned on the charm and did everything to monopolize Ellie's attention. Brady thought it amusing at first, then became uncomfortable as through the course of the evening Ellie and Cal were revealed to share a number of common interests as well.

That Cal had leaned over to him with his observations when Ellie disappeared into the kitchen with a pile of dirty plates furthered the discomfort.

"She's terrific, Brady. Brains, looks, sense of humor, she's the whole damn package."

"I know she is." *She's mine.*

Cal nodded toward the kitchen. "Is it serious between you two?"

"Very." Brady was blunt.

"So I shouldn't bother to wait around until you fuck up, eh?"

Brady smirked. "I don't intend to this time, my friend. Though I should warn you, Ellie's the adventurous type. She's up for a bit of fun."

Cal smiled. "What are we talking, kayaking on the bay fun or Room 112 fun?" Room 112 had been the hotel room number where Brady and Cal enjoyed their one and only three-way so many years ago. It was their code when talking about that particular adventure.

"What do you think?"

Cal nodded; he needed no further explanation. "Just say when. It's gonna be like Christmas morning."

"Cal, you were raised Jewish."

"Hey, I never said I was observant."

Cal was certainly observant of Ellie, Brady recalled of that night, and of the days following whenever the three were together.

Now, after several weeks of recording and rehearsing, mixing tracks and glad-handling regional TV and radio contacts for publicity, Dareville had a sold-out benefit concert starring Brady Garriston to put on the next night. And as reward for all their hard work and preparation, tonight he was going to make one more fantasy for Ellie come true.

He emerged from the master bathroom, clad only in a towel tied around his waist, to see Ellie sitting cross-legged on his bed. She was wearing her green silk robe, tied loosely enough so that he could still see her breasts peeking from the fabric. The scene surprised him somewhat, as Ellie normally was wont to rip off her clothes the second she stepped into his house, even with Cal bunking in the guest bedroom for the duration of his stay.

"Are you cold?" he asked. The towel dropped to the carpet, and he smiled at the look on Ellie's face as she beheld his body. It never got old.

"I'm fine." She nodded, toying with the thin belt of her robe. "Just a little nervous."

"Why?" He rounded the bed and slid behind her. He massaged her shoulders and moved away a lock of hair to kiss her neck. "We're not to going to be doing anything you haven't done before."

"I know, it's just that I'm going to be doing it with two men at once." Ellie did not resist when Brady reached around her to peel the robe away from her shoulders, revealing her taut, creamy breasts. "I know I've talked about wanting to do it, and now the time's come I guess I'm a bit scared."

Brady had to laugh at that. This from a woman who, only days prior, had purposely not worn panties underneath her sundress and bent over a fruit display at Jake's Market to give him a view of something sweeter. Never mind that a pack of nuns could have paraded past on their way to the deli.

"You don't have anything to worry about. Cal's a good guy, and he's not going to do anything you don't want him to do. You like him, right?"

"Oh, Cal's great. I love him to death."

Brady's smile fell slack.

"He's a great catch. I'm surprised some woman hasn't snatched him right up."

"Cal's not the type to let himself be caught." Though Brady worried whether or not Cal would slow down if Ellie ran after him. "Do you think

163

you could go for him?" he ventured cautiously, and felt some relief when Ellie immediately shook her head.

"He's attractive and all, with a great body, but he doesn't do to me what you do." She leaned back and nipped Brady on the lips. "He doesn't make my blood boil."

Brady's own blood surged, his apprehensions about tonight fading. Yes, Cal was a very handsome man, and rivaled, if not exceeded, him in sexual prowess. They had been close friends for decades, yet Brady would not put it past his friend, either, if he tried to woo Ellie away. Hearing Ellie now put him at ease.

"I guess I'm just…" Ellie's voice trailed off as Brady cupped her breasts and rolled her nipples between his fingers. "Oh, that's nice. Maybe you're right. I'm just over-thinking this whole thing."

"Atta girl." Though deep inside, Brady did not blame her for feeling nervous. A third party in sex was a big step. Perhaps he would only allow this to happen once.

He drew Ellie closer and nuzzled her neck, kissing her ear and temple. Ellie giggled her appreciation. "I am excited, too, so you know," Ellie told him. "Sooner or later, we'll have to find a nice girl to join us for some fun, too."

Brady arched an eyebrow. Perhaps not yet.

"Where *is* Cal, anyway?"

Brady did not answer immediately, but continued kissing a trail down Ellie's neck and shoulder. If he knew his friend, Cal was sitting out on the backyard patio, smoking a joint. Brady had given up the stuff years ago, and did not want it in the house with Ellie, who was strictly anti-drug. "He's around," he answered finally. "Probably engaged in his usual pre-sex rituals."

"What?" Ellie laughed. "What rituals? Lighting an oblation to the sex gods in thanks?"

"Not quite."

This came from Cal, who had appeared in the doorway, also clad in a short robe. Brady acknowledged his friend with a slight nod, and watched Ellie take in Cal's tall, lean frame, light brown hair pulled back in a long ponytail, and hazel eyes. The slight smile on his lips gave him a boyish, mischievous look, one Brady easily identified with his friend. Cal was going to enjoy himself, Brady knew, and would make sure Ellie did.

"Hey there," Ellie called to him.

"Hey yourself," Cal said. "You look good enough to eat."

"What about me?" Brady asked.

Cal snorted, and Ellie laughed. Moving away from Brady, she let her robe fall completely from her body as she lay back on the bed. Brady followed suit and molded against her right side, his cock stiffening against her hip. Cal, meanwhile, wasted no pretense and dropped his own robe to reveal a nearly airborne cock as big as Brady's. He was snug against Ellie's left side within seconds.

Brady detected the sweet aroma of marijuana on Cal as his friend bent slightly to kiss Ellie on the lips. A swift pang of jealousy roiled his stomach as Ellie's lips parted and eagerly returned the kiss, but he kept it in check. Ellie was his, he had to remind himself. She was not going anywhere. She had said Cal did not attract her the way he did. There was no reason to get upset.

"So what do you want?" Brady asked Ellie.

Ellie turned to him with a lazy smile. "I want to feel two mouths sucking on my tits."

Neither man saw a problem with that, and each bent his head down to capture an erect nipple and suckle hard. Brady's heart thrummed with Ellie's every moan; he knew she was watching them through the ceiling tiles, and he could not resist a quick peek himself. Cal's eyes were closed as he laved Ellie's breast, his hand resting on Ellie's abdomen. Brady reached down to stroke Ellie's pussy, intensifying her vocal appreciation, and he watched as she reached from her sides to cuff an erection in each hand and stroke upward.

He heard Cal's breathing quicken along with his. Ellie's hand movements were identical; she stroked each shaft, rotating a thumb pad around the tip of each cock and spreading what precum threatened to spill.

"I can't decide which one of these magnificent cocks I want to suck first," she said.

Cal released his hold on her nipple. "I am a guest in this house, you know."

"Flip a coin," Brady quipped.

"Paper, rock, scissors?" Cal joked back.

"You cheat at that."

Ellie quivered underneath him, more from laughter than erotic pleasure. "Okay, guys. Just for that, we go in alphabetical order. Brady." She turned to him again and beckoned him to a more accessible position.

"What can I do in the meantime?" Cal asked, his voice near pouting.

Ellie's answer was to raise her knees and spread them so far apart that her pussy lips parted on their own. Cal smiled; he needed no further invitation, and slithered to the foot of the bed. As Brady reclined against the headboard, Ellie twisted her upper body so she could take his cock into her mouth, while Cal dipped his head over Ellie's pussy, pried her cleft apart with two fingers, and lapped at her moistened folds.

"That's so good," Brady muttered. His eyes darted back and forth, alternating between watching Ellie eat him and Cal eating Ellie. It was a familiar sight, one evoking memories of the last and only other time he and Cal had tag-teamed a woman. But that was different. That woman had no name and, as time wore on, had a face so insignificant that its features were fading. They had been young boys out for fun then, and while this *was* also fun it held deeper meaning. Here, Brady had set out to show Ellie that he would do anything for her, because he loved her.

Yes, he had to admit it. He loved Ellie, and wanted her for always. Even if it meant having to share her once in a while.

He gazed down at her body, her beautiful white skin and luscious curves, her tensing thighs sandwiching Cal's face as his tongue stroked her clit in a figure-eight motion, soon driving her body into a shuddering orgasm. He watched her come, watched Cal lap at her slit to drink up her juices.

167

Her face contorted, his cock still throbbing in her mouth as she intensified the suction. He stroked her cheek; she looked so damn beautiful.

But he did not want to come in her mouth. He wanted to be where Cal was, but Cal was not quite ready to relinquish his position. His friend rose abruptly and reached over him for the box on the nightstand, plucking a condom from it. He watched Cal roll the Latex sheath down his thick erection before positioning the tip at the entrance of Ellie's slick opening.

"You ready for me?" Cal's breathing was heavy.

Ellie, her mouth still occupied with Brady's cock, nodded, and exhaled sharply when Cal first scraped the reservoir tip of the condom against her opening before ramming his cock to the hilt. Brady felt the spasm at the other end and cried out. It felt as if Ellie had tried to bite off his cock.

"Easy now," he cooed, stroking her hair. "It doesn't grow back."

Ellie released her oral hold and smiled complacently at him. "Sorry," she whispered, and licked his shaft from top to bottom before resuming her deep-throated pace, set in time now to Cal's every thrust inside her.

Brady closed his eyes and tilted his head back, enjoying the sensation as Ellie's lips tightened around him, though Cal's periodic grunts were fast becoming a distraction. He couldn't bear open his eyes, though, and watch Cal stroking into Ellie's pussy. The longest two minutes of his life passed.

"Okay, I can't take this anymore," he finally grunted, and eased Ellie's head up his shaft until she was clear. "I need to be inside you now."

"You just were," Cal said, looking up from her.

"Yeah," Ellie pouted, then smiled. All previous worries of the evening had disappeared from her face, washed away in a wave of orgasm.

Brady reached behind him for the box on his nightstand and pulled out two condoms. "You know what I mean."

Seconds later, both men were sheathed with fresh condoms and Ellie was straddling Brady's hips, settling herself onto his cock. She bent over and kissed Brady, brushing her nipples against his. Cal, kneeling behind her, smoothed one hand up and down her concave back while he used the other to lubricate her anal opening with lotion. Occasionally he bent forward to plant kisses down her spine.

"Having fun?" Brady whispered in her ear when Ellie's face lowered to his.

"Uh-huh." Her voice was evident of her enthusiasm. Her pussy clamped around him as she rocked slowly against him, sending a shockwave through his system.

"You ready?"

She sucked in breath through her teeth, her face suddenly serious. She turned back to Cal, now kneading her buttocks, and nodded.

"Now," she whispered.

Cal nodded, and gently spread her cheeks and pressed the tip of his cock against her anus.

"Don't worry," he said. "Cal's going to take good care of you." With that, he eased himself slowly into her. Brady nearly laughed at the expression on Ellie's as she turned back to face him. They were truly going to be okay, he knew. No way could Ellie become enamored with a guy who referred to himself in the third person.

The light-hearted moment, however, quickly gave way to a soaring passion. Ellie straightened her body as much as possible, allowing both men to sandwich her. She rocked against Brady's cock, while Cal pumped gently in and out of her tighter opening. Ellie arched her neck back and closed her eyes, letting both men kiss and caress her. Occasionally Brady's touch would overstep the boundary and extend to Cal, but his friend did not protest. In fact, Cal appeared to encourage the ministrations, a fact evident when Cal boldly grabbed hold of one of Brady's hands and placed it firmly against his ass.

Okay. Brady had never before touched his friend like this, and to his surprise he was not put off. At least Cal had a nice ass for touching. He squeezed tightly, prompting Cal to increase his thrusts into Ellie, to her audible delight.

Briefly, then, came the thought of what it would be like to thrust his cock into that nice ass. Ellie would not mind watching that, he was certain.

This thought was confirmed when he craned his head to one side, his eyes fixed on Cal. The two locked gazes, breathing heavy. As if agreeing to some unspoken communication, they met each other halfway and locked lips, plundering each other's mouths with abandon. The light stubble on Cal's upper lip scratched at his own, but the sensation was hardly unpleasant. The taste of marijuana and Ellie was strong, and he delighted in it.

Ellie's approving murmurs tickled Brady's ear. "Ooh, bad boys," she teased. "You gonna do more for me later?"

Brady broke free of the kiss and planted one on Ellie's cheek. "Right now I'm gonna come."

"Hang on," Cal growled. His torso slapped against Ellie's ass. "We'll come together."

And they did, the three of them, in harmonious crescendo.

And Brady and Ellie looked at each other, sweating and gasping for breath, yet each managing to say the same thing.

"I love you."

* * *

As much as she wanted to stay, and both men wholeheartedly encouraged her to do so, Ellie insisted on spending the rest of the night alone at her apartment. Though tomorrow was Saturday, it was the day of the concert, and she knew if she stayed nobody would get the rest needed for the big event.

Not that she could sleep anyway, alone or with two gorgeous men flanking her. She was floating on air, basking in the most erotic experience of her life. And Brady had told her he loved her!

How in the hell were she and Brady going to

top that? Sex on the Goodyear Blimp? The White House lawn? The space shuttle?

As she drove the short distance back to her complex, she wondered if Brady and Cal, too, would be getting any sleep at all following their three-way tryst. Both seemed rather keyed up in the afterglow. It would not surprise her if the two decided to go a second round without her.

A smile of regret touched her lips. If Brady and Cal were making love right now, she wanted to witness it. Seeing their brief kiss had sparked something inside her—not jealousy or anger, but a feeling that had enhanced the moment. It turned her on to see Brady kissing another man, and he had admitted to doing more in the past. Maybe, if they had another man join them again, if Cal joined them again, she could encourage the two males to participate more with each other. To see them in passionate embrace, kissing and sucking each other...

She shifted in the driver's seat and applied the brakes. She was going to come right there on the corner of Main and Maple if she was not careful, and plow her car right into Jake's Market.

There was a strange car parked in her second space, she saw as she slowed her car into her small apartment complex. Virginia plates. Perhaps one of her neighbors had company? It was possible, as everybody in the building knew she lived alone, and she had allowed others free reign of the space if needed.

But there was somebody dozing in the driver's

seat, a woman with her head turned to the other side. Ellie parked and exited her car, her heart beating faster as she rounded the front and instantly recognized her surprise guest.

"Claire!"

THIRTEEN

What the hell was Claire doing here? Why wasn't she in New York?

Ellie put a hand to her mouth. Claire had found out about her and Brady, and had come here...to do what? Break them up? Why would she? Claire had made it clear she wanted nothing more to do with Brady.

At least, Claire had *said* that. Maybe she was lying.

There could be no other explanation for her presence here, but how did she know to come? Tomorrow's concert had not been advertised outside of the region. Had there been a leak in the media? Lauren did not know where to contact Claire, either, unless the two had been conversing without her knowledge.

Claire was slumped in the driver's seat, dozing with her arms folded. Ellie's cry of surprise was loud enough to jar her awake, and she looked momentarily dazed until she caught sight of her slack-jawed cousin standing just outside the rental car.

Claire stumbled out of the car and took her cousin into a fierce hug. "Where have you been?" she cried. "I've been sitting in that damn car for nearly an hour!"

Ellie patted her cousin's back, but quickly drew away. She smelled of sex and a lethal combination of Cal's and Brady's colognes, and the last thing she needed was for Claire to question it.

Claire looked equally disheveled in a gray business suit, wrinkled with wear and travel, her hair frizzed. Red, raw skin lined her eyes.

The questions came at once. "What are you doing here?" Ellie wanted to know. "When did you arrive? Why didn't you let me know you were coming, and why did you wait out here? You have a key to my place."

She helped a loping Claire into the apartment. Her cousin flopped backward onto the couch and kicked off her heels, reclining her legs. "My key's back at my apartment," she groaned, "and I haven't been home today. I just hopped in a cab, went to LaGuardia, and hopped the first flight I could get to Norfolk. Rented a car, drove here. No luggage, no nothing." Ellie saw fresh tears shine in Claire's eyes.

"Claire," she said, softly this time, "what happened?"

"No self-respect, no life, either," Claire wailed, and looked up her cousin mournfully. "I needed to see a friendly face. You're my best friend, the only person I can talk to."

"Claire." Ellie's heart went out to her cousin. Whatever happened must have been bad, and she knew she had to give Claire the time to talk on her own.

Typhoid took the cue to pounce into Claire's lap and purr loudly. Claire bundled the cat into her arms and nuzzled into her fur.

"Hey, Ty," Claire whispered.

"Do you want some tea?" Ellie offered. "Or coffee?"

"I'd rather have a drink."

"I have vodka and cranberry. How about I make two martinis?"

Claire rested her head against a pillow and let Typhoid squirm from her grasp. "Sounds good. Make yourself two while you're at it."

Halfway into her third Cosmopolitan, Claire's tongue loosened enough to talk.

"The guy I've been seeing," Claire began.

"Roger?"

"Robert," Claire corrected her. "And no, he's ancient history. This was Antoine. We'd been seeing each other a few weeks, and I thought for sure he was the one for me."

"What told you differently?" Ellie could already guess, though.

"Not what, whom. *Mrs.* Antoine." A broad gesture caused a drop of Claire's martini to fly into the air. "She comes barging into my office this afternoon, screaming in Italian. I think I recognized the words "whore" and "murder" before building security carried her away." Claire's chest heaved. "Everybody in the office is looking at me, and I'm so embarrassed I just got the hell out of there."

"Claire." Ellie set down her glass and took her cousin in her arms. "I'm so sorry that happened to you. But it's not your fault. You didn't know Antoine was married, did you?"

Claire shook her head. "I feel like I'm jinxed.

Every man I've gone out with since I dumped Brady has turned out to be either a liar or a total loser. And these are men who are the complete opposite of him, you know? Stable men, or so I thought, with jobs like mine. Men *I've* been trying to find for a lasting relationship."

Ellie nodded. She did not like where this conversation was headed.

"So I'm standing in the middle of Wall Street on my cell phone, trying to hail a cab," Claire continued. "At that moment it came to me that you were right all along."

"I was?" Ellie was confused. "How?"

"Remember a few months ago when you said I still had it bad for Brady? You were right." Claire lowered her gaze and stared into her empty glass. "I did then and I think I do now. I didn't think he was my type. I thought Brady was too immature for a stable relationship, and it turns out that's he the most stable man I've ever dated."

Ellie touched a hand to her fluttering heart. She agreed. Wild as he acted at times, he had everything together.

"I guess I was intimidated by his attitude, you know?" Claire continued. "Equating spontaneity with childish behavior, but you were right. There's no difference. I mean, I just hopped on a flight from New York, I guess I can be spontaneous, too."

"No difference, spontaneous," Ellie echoed. Her mind conjured the memory of Brady against her, on top of her, inside her.

"So, I called Brady's apartment on the chance

that he would be there and would want to talk, and you know what I found out?"

Ellie swallowed back some vodka-flavored vomit. Her heart swelled to the point of bursting. "What?" It was a great chore to say that one word in a calm voice.

Claire smirked and threw up her hands. "His daughter answered. She's apartment sitting for him. Told me Brady took off again, and didn't tell anybody where, not even her. He wanted to get away to work on his next album. He could be anywhere."

"Well." Ellie let go of Claire and inched to the other end of the couch. "In his defense, you told him you wanted to move on, and maybe he decided to do the same. I mean, he had no idea to expect this to happen, he wasn't going to ask your permission to leave town."

"Yeah," Claire conceded. "I just wish I knew where he was. I looked up his friend, some bass player he works with, and he's not in town either."

No. That Cal was not. Ellie bit her lip. "Hey, they're musicians, right?" She tried to keep her voice light. "Maybe they're recording in LA." *Yeah, you could try LA. I'll drive you to the airport right now and get you on a plane.*

Claire sighed. "I really fucked up when I dumped him, El," he said. "If I could just find him and talk to him, maybe we could work it out. Not necessarily pick up where we left off, but maybe start again a bit more slowly. I'd get to know him better before I made any more rash judgments."

Ellie's shoulders sagged. Who was she kidding? The Norfolk airport had no flights leaving at this hour. She was stuck with Claire at least until morning.

Or all time, she realized. What good would it do to send her back to New York? Claire would keep calling Brady's place there, and eventually Brady was going to have to go back. No, Claire would have to be told the truth, and soon. Ellie could only imagine the ensuing fireworks.

But...what if Brady decided to go back to Claire? Would he do that, after telling her that he loved her? He had not said that to Claire when they were dating, though he was probably on the verge of doing so. Would all his words of how he preferred her to Claire be forgotten the second he learned Claire wanted him back?

"Oh, God," Claire cried, and her hand came down hard on Ellie's shoulder, startling her. "I've been having this pity party here, and I haven't let you talk." She sniffled loudly. "So," her voice turned cheery, "were you on a date tonight? Is that why you're home so late?"

"Uh, yeah. I was." Ellie willed the memories of her threesome to the forefront, wondering if that would be all she would have left by weekend's end. Memories.

"Still seeing that Garth guy?"

"Gary," Ellie said. *Brady. I'm seeing Brady now, you can't have him back. He loves me.* "Yes, we are still seeing each other."

Claire leaned over and hugged her close. "Well, I'm glad one of us is doing good in the men's department. Maybe I'll get to meet him this weekend?"

Ellie said nothing.

Claire sobered. "I *can* stay, right? I have to fly back Sunday, but I really need to be away from the city right now."

"Of course you can stay. Don't be silly, I would never turn you out." The words were acid in Ellie's mouth, but what else could she say? Claire was family, her best friend, and she knew her longer than she did Brady. Claire took precedence despite her love for Brady, despite her longing to be forever wrapped in his arms, stroking the fine muscles of his arms and back, making love with him...

Stop it.

Abruptly Claire jumped from the couch. "Man, I have to pee," she said, wincing. "I've held it in since New York." And, knowing where everything in Ellie's apartment was, she bolted for the bathroom in the master suite. No sooner than the door closed behind Claire, the phone rang, preventing Ellie from absorbing their conversation.

Only one person could be calling her this late. Ellie dashed to the kitchen and picked up the slim wall phone before a second ring could prompt Claire's curiosity. Her greeting to Brady was breathless.

"Come over now," he said.

"Brady," she chided, and lowered her voice. "Come on, you need your rest. You have a big day tomorrow."

"Why are we whispering?" Brady whispered

back, playful.

"I, uh, don't want to wake the cat." Ellie hope it would sound enough like a lame joke for Brady to want to play along. It must have worked, because he laughed.

"I want some pussy, and I don't mean Ty." His voice turned husky. The sensation shot right through Ellie's head down to her toes, warming her all over.

"You know I want to be there, too, honey," Ellie said. She did want to be there. She wanted to be in bed with him right now, kissing every inch of his bare body, regardless of whether or not Cal participated, watched them, or watched television in the next room. That was much preferable to her current situation and the doubtful thoughts swirling in her head.

"So why aren't you here?" Brady asked. "Come back. I got a hard on that won't quit until you get here, and come."

"I'm not going to be held responsible when you show up at the concert and fall asleep at the piano," Ellie said, firmly yet lovingly.

"S'alright. We'll blame Cal." Ellie could hear Cal laughing in the background. She wondered what they were doing, what they had been doing. Were they still naked? Oh, she *so* wanted to be there instead of babysitting the blubbering cousin who could ruin her life!

"Hey," Brady prodded. "Guess what Cal's doing right now."

"He should be going to sleep, too."

"He's sucking my cock." Brady moaned. "You should be here, girl. It feels so good, but he's not as good at it as you are." In the background, Ellie heard Cal jokingly exclaim, "Oh, thanks."

Ellie had a clear picture in her mind of it. Unconsciously a hand fell to her crotch to still the throbbing in her pussy. Yes, she did want to see that, if Brady was not bluffing. "You guys are impossible."

"And when he's done, I'm gonna suck his. Don't you want to see that?"

Mama. Why were the sex gods taunting her tonight? "Good night, boys," she sang, masking the pain in her voice.

"Come over," Brady begged.

"Go to sleep."

"Tuck me in."

"Let Cal do it."

"Tuck me, fuck me, suck me." She heard Brady gasp, then there were some indistinguishable noises. Maybe they were not bluffing after all. Why couldn't Claire have stayed in New York and tried one more boring guy to date?

"Brady." Her voice was firm, yet her body quaked with want and grief.

There was a pause, then, in a boyish voice, "No?"

"No."

"After the show, then? We'll blow off your friend Lauren, maybe hook her up with Cal, and you and I can have a nice, quiet dinner alone."

"Of course, I'd love that." Tears welled in her

eyes. Would there really be an after the show for them?

"I love you," Brady told her.

"I love you, too. Goodnight." And Ellie rang off before either could say anything more, before Brady could hear her start to cry. Quietly she slumped to the kitchen floor and buried her face in her hands, pressing her fingers into her eyes to keep the tears from spilling.

Why did this have to happen? Why did Brady have to choose here to start over, and why did she have to fall in love with him? The old adage was truthful, be careful what you wish for because you just might get it. And Ellie had wished for an exciting man, got one, and now stood to lose him if Claire was indeed serious about wanting Brady back.

She stood. *No.* Claire had her chance, and yes, she blew it. Brady loved *her*. Surely his spontaneous nature did not extend to declaring love the way a person might order takeout. Claire had to know that. She had to know that "Gary" was really Brady.

She listened. It was awfully quiet in the apartment.

"Claire?" She stepped into the bedroom. Apparently Claire had done her business in the master bath, because now she was collapsed on the bed, snoring into a pillow with Typhoid curled at her stocking feet.

"Claire," Ellie moaned. She wondered if her cousin would wake up tomorrow and wonder where she was. Rather than wake her, she shifted

Claire's body so that she lay entirely on the bed, then covered her with an extra blanket. Slipping off her clothes for a nightgown, she slid under the covers of the unoccupied side and closed her eyes, wondering what morning would bring.

FOURTEEN

Something wasn't right.

Brady had gone for a bike ride early Saturday morning and returned home to a message on his machine from Ellie. She sounded upset; Typhoid was not well, and she was taking him to a vet in Virginia Beach since Dareville did not have one. She did not know long the trip would take, and she would see him tonight at the park before the concert.

That had been nearly ten hours ago, and he had not heard from her since. Ellie did not have a cell phone, and he did not know how to contact her. One thing he did know for certain was that the vet story was bullshit. An afternoon drive past her complex revealed a perfectly healthy Typhoid sitting in the front window of her apartment, and Ellie's car was still in her space. Nobody answered when he knocked, and a quick check through the patio glass doors revealed the place was empty.

Something was definitely not right.

Now, with an hour before showtime, Brady did not know what to do or what to think. Ellie's mysterious disappearance preyed on his mind throughout the day, and it was certain to affect his performance if she didn't show up soon. During his last rehearsal that afternoon he had flubbed a few lines of one of his biggest songs. He could not afford to mess up tonight; too many people were counting on the success of this show.

Ellie had been counting on him. She was reason he had agreed to do this damn show. *Where was she?*

It frustrated him, too, that he could not talk to Cal about it, because Cal was also acting strange. True to last night's phone call to Ellie, he and Cal had continued to fool around after she left. Whether it was a result of fired up hormones or the pot Cal had smoked, his friend had willingly sucked his cock, and Brady reciprocated. It had been the first time ever that he had given a man a blowjob, and he enjoyed it. Cal's shaft was thick, and his skin soft and warm as it slid effortlessly in and out of his mouth. He had felt a great deal of satisfaction when Cal's breath hitched and released a bellowing orgasm as he shot his load into Brady's mouth. Brady drained him, watching the ecstasy flutter across his friend's face. Cal had looked so beautiful then.

After waking up in each other's arms that morning, however, Cal slipped quietly out of bed, into the shower, and said nothing about the incident.

In fact, Cal had said not one word to him all day, only communicated through shrugs and nods. Last night everybody had been fine, and had enjoyed themselves. What changed?

Brady paced the interior of the Airstream trailer he rented, at his own expense to defray costs to the town and building fund, to use for his dressing room. It was parked behind the stage area at the park, and Lauren was going to come by just before curtain to fetch him for the show. He wondered now if that would be a good idea, if he would not just go out there and royally fuck up his performance, forget how to play the piano, and earn the ire of all ticket holders and fans.

Ironic. He had come to quiet, unassuming Dareville to rejuvenate his career, and now it looked as though the place would be the death of it.

Abruptly he stopped; his heart pounded wildly in his ribcage. What if Ellie had not called because she could not call? What if she had gone somewhere with a friend—shopping at the beach, someplace to get something for tonight, like a new dress to surprise him—and got into an accident? What if she was lying unconscious in some emergency room, hooked up to tubes and machines? Nobody would know to contact him.

No. The thought of Ellie seriously injured, or near death, made him nauseous, yet it was enough to propel him to the door. Screw the concert, the school, the town. Ellie meant more to him. He had to find out for sure that she was all right, even if he had to drive to every hospital in the state.

He flung open the door to find Cal standing on the wrought iron steps, his fist poised to knock, his expression bewildered. "Where's the fire?" he asked.

Brady slumped against the threshold. "He speaks," he bit out. "Get out of my way."

"Show's starting in an hour, and we have a

sound check. You can't go anywhere."

"I'll do what I damn well please," Brady shouted, and tried to push past Cal. His friend, however, was too strong for him. Cal soon had him by the collarbone, and pushed him deep into the trailer, forcing Brady onto a narrow couch. Cal stood over him, arms crossed, as if expecting retaliation, but Brady suddenly felt too aggrieved to offer any. Instead he cradled his head in his hands.

"Where the fuck is Ellie?" he asked, his voice near choking.

"She'll be here. Don't get so worked up. Here." Cal bent into an adjacent micro-refrigerator and pulled out two beers, handing one to Brady.

"She lied to me about the damn vet, took off with somebody else." Brady wrenched the cap from the brown beer bottle and pitched it across the trailer.

Cal sat next to him and took a long pull from his own bottle. "She probably went shopping with a friend and lost track of time," he suggested. "Or got stuck in traffic, and it's taking a while."

"It doesn't take ten hours to go shopping."

"Girl's gotta eat."

"She could be on the side of the road with a flat," Brady said, frowning. "She could be lying dead in some ditch—"

"She's fine," Cal said forcefully. "She will be here. She wouldn't ditch you like this."

Brady scowled a sideways glance at his friend. "You don't know that. You barely know Ellie." *But you fucked her, and I let you.* He questioned the wisdom of that decision now. It was what she wanted, though, and he wanted what she wanted. Now, he wondered if that was the reason she had taken off like she did. Maybe the three-way had been too overwhelming for her. Maybe his phone call later spooked her somehow. It would certainly explain how oddly she had sounded on the phone.

Cal leaned back against the couch, stretching his long legs in front of him. "No, I don't know her very well," he agreed, "but I consider myself a fairly perceptive guy. If there's one thing I do know, it's that Ellie loves you."

Brady cast Cal a withering look, which was immediately waved away. "Don't give me that," Cal scolded. "I've seen the way she looks at you, the way she talks to you. Who was she looking at the whole time we were all together last night? It wasn't me."

Brady said nothing.

Cal took another long swallow and smirked. "I saw the look on your face last night when I was eating her, and fucking her pussy. You didn't care much for me doing that, did you?"

Brady had to admit he did not. He didn't like seeing another man bringing Ellie to orgasm. He wanted that privilege, and Ellie's pussy, for himself.

"Last night wasn't really about me. It was what Ellie wanted," he said.

Cal nodded and looked away. "I noticed, too, Ellie didn't seem to mind that the evening ended so soon. Yeah, she got what she wanted, but I really think that was for you to admit that you loved her. If I'm not mistaken, she'll come tonight. Have some faith."

I hope you're right. But Brady did not say it loud. He finished his beer, and Cal produced another one for him. The two sat quietly, drinking and not looking at each other, Brady trying to mellow.

Eventually Cal spoke again. "About what happened later last night, and why I haven't said anything—"

"Yeah?" Brady picked at the dampened label of his bottle.

"It's not something I'd do often, or ever again, but I'm glad it was with you."

Brady nodded. There was no point in saying more, and embarrassing his friend. They remained silent for several more minutes, until a knock on the door alerted them to a young man with a clipboard, who requested their presence for the final sound check before showtime.

Minutes before he was to go on, Ellie had yet to arrive. By then the park was near bursting with people. The premier seats—twenty rows of folding chairs close to the stage—were nearly occupied, while everybody else had set up blankets on the back lawn. All, however, were standing and cheering on Cal and the rest of the band as they warmed up with an instrumental version of one of Brady's songs. Brady stood in the wings, watching the crowd, in particular one empty chair in the front row.

"Nervous?"

Brady whirled around, startled. Lauren was standing just behind him, a laminated backstage pass hanging from her neck by a thick red cord. His face fell. For a second she sounded like Ellie.

"I'll be okay, everything seems to be set well. Sound's good," he said without enthusiasm.

"I know you've heard me say this a thousand times in the past few weeks, but thank you so much for doing this," Lauren said. "After paying off the bills to put this on, the profit is still more than enough to fix the school. We are so grateful, too, that you pitched in to help with some of the expenses."

"I'm glad." Brady could have cared less about the tax write-off he stood to receive, or the school, just one of its faculty. "I only wish Ellie shared the sentiment."

"Ellie?" Lauren frowned and pointed toward the crowd. "Why wouldn't she? She's got the best seat in the house."

"Huh?" And Brady turned back toward the crowd, his eyes widening with disbelief.

* * *

Ellie checked her watch for the thousandth time. She was half-surprised Claire had not yet questioned this nervous tic and teased her about being late for a hot date with "Gary." Claire had said nothing at all about Dareville, or wanting to go back, and for that Ellie was relieved.

But Claire talked much of Brady, which only reinforced her pain. She had had Claire drive them to the beach to distract her with sightseeing and shopping, but everything seemed to remind her cousin of Brady. Brady would have liked the beach, Brady would have loved eating here for lunch, do you think Brady would like this dress, Claire had asked her more than once.

She watched Claire frown and return the last dress to its rack before guiding Ellie out of the fifteenth boutique they visited. "Why am I asking you that?" she asked. "You never met Brady."

Ellie sighed inwardly. *If you only knew.* She strapped on her seatbelt. "Where to now?"

Claire yawned and cranked the engine. "Home. I'm beat. I think we've hit every store on the shore, anyway." She shrugged in the T-shirt she had borrowed from Ellie, which fit a bit too tightly. "Besides, I don't have any luggage to take home all this stuff I bought."

"We could go to the mall," Ellie suggested. "There's a travel shop there. We could get you a bag." It was close to six now; the concert was due to start at seven. Brady was probably worried sick or steaming mad that she had not called him all day, but after ten hours she could still not think of what to say to him. The best plan she could come up with, lame as it was, was to get Claire out of town, wear her to exhaustion, and hope she slept the rest of the evening while she slipped away to catch at least the second half of the show. With any luck, Claire would never know Brady was in town, and she would be off to Norfolk in the morning to fly home, being none the wiser.

Then she would have to convince Brady to sell his place in New York and never, ever return there. They could move to Europe, change their names...

Right.

Ellie fought back a lump growing in her throat as Claire's rental car pulled onto the highway leading back to Dareville. Traffic was light, so most certainly they would be home sooner than expected. "So you're tired, huh?" Ellie prodded. "I'll bet you just want to kick back on the couch and fall asleep."

"I could use the rest, yeah," Claire agreed, and Ellie relaxed. She tightened up again, however, when Claire spoke again.

"Is Gary coming by? I'd like to meet him."

"Uh, no. He had to work today." Ellie bit her lip. It was not a complete lie. "I'm going to meet him up at Mick's just after I freshen up."

Claire nodded. Ellie knew that Claire had enjoyed going to Mick's Restaurant, the nicest eatery in Dareville, though it was dry.

"Maybe I could tag along? Don't they usually have a band on Saturday nights? I might run into some old friends."

"No! I mean; you don't want to do that," Ellie said nervously as Claire cast her a look. "I mean, not many of the old gang hangs out there anymore, they usually go into Suffolk for the evening, and I don't want you to feel like a third wheel." She shifted in her seat. "You know, I could cancel with Gary. You and I could rent a movie and hang out at home."

It pained her to say those words. To do that would mean missing the show. What would Brady think when he learned she never showed up?

Then again, maybe it was for the best. If Brady

got the idea that she was no longer interested, it would ease Claire's eventual reunion with him. It was bound to happen. They were both New Yorkers, both in a similar societal and financial class. She was just a small-town schoolteacher, making the most of a sexual summer camp, as it were.

"You'd do that?" Claire asked, surprised, then shook her head. "No, I can't let you do that. Just because my love life is shit doesn't mean it has to transcend yours. Go out with Gary, have a good time. I'll be fine at home."

Ellie shook her head. Claire was not going to be fine until she confronted Brady once and for all. None of them were, and when it did happen somebody was still not going to be fine. She had been wrong to prolong the inevitable, she realized.

They were only a few miles outside the town limits. The traffic thickened suddenly on the highway, with a stream of cars heading in the same direction. Claire frowned.

"What's going on tonight? I've never seen so many cars."

Ellie pointed to a back road leading to the park. "Turn here."

"Why? That road doesn't go to the apartment."

Ellie unzipped her purse and pulled out a hanging parking pass, given to her by Brady to use for tonight's VIP parking. "Just do it, please?" she said. "There's something I need to show you, something I should have told you a long time ago."

Claire shrugged but did not protest. She followed Ellie's directions until they were parking beside a short row of cars near an Airstream trailer situated at one end of the park. As far as the eye could see, there were people milling around, many scurrying through one main entrance with blankets and coolers and children in tow. A huge stage setup blocked their view of the crowd. Claire marveled at it all as Ellie led her down the opposite path to a more private entrance.

"What's going on, some kind of festival?" Claire asked.

"A benefit, for the school. Somebody you know is headlining." Ellie saw Lauren standing watch at the VIP gate. The other woman, upon recognizing Claire, dashed over to give her a hug.

"Wow!" Lauren exclaimed. "I never expected to see *you* here."

"It's kind of a last minute visit," Claire began, but Ellie cut them both off before either one could go into detail. She handed Lauren fifty dollars.

"Can Claire could stay with me for the show?"

"Sure, no problem." Lauren waved them through the VIP entrance, close to the stage. As they rounded the corner, Ellie caught sight of Cal jamming a bass solo to the crowd's delight. He did not see her creeping down the front row with Claire to the last unoccupied seat.

"Ellie!" Claire had to shout to be heard over the speakers. "What the hell's going on?" Further words died in her throat as her gaze turned toward the stage. "Is that—?"

Ellie confirmed Claire's shock with a sad nod,

and both watched as Brady strode confidently to his piano, waving and nodding to the appreciative crowd.

He looked absolutely sexy, dressed in tight black jeans and a green DPA T-shirt that accentuated his biceps and chest. As he walked upstage he seemed to acknowledge everybody in the front row with a dazzling smile, and when he neared where Ellie and Claire stood his gaze appeared all the more smoldering and sensual.

Claire stood openmouthed at first, then squealed with delight. Ellie could only stare back, wondering who that smile was for as Brady took to the piano and launched immediately into the first song.

Claire had her by the shoulders now. The heat of the crowd was stifling, the music stabbed at her heart. "What's he doing here? How did this happen?" she cried.

"I contacted him on my own," Ellie lied. "The DPA Building Committee knew you two had dated, and we thought we'd take a shot at getting him to perform a benefit for the school fund. I explained who I was and what we needed. We had no idea he'd say yes."

"He did this, for the school?" Claire gasped, then shook his head. "No, there has to be more than that."

There is more. He did this for me.

"He did this for me," Claire cried, jubilant. "He wanted to prove his love for me, so when you contacted him and told him who you were, he agreed to do it for me, I'll bet. Oh, Ellie!" She hugged her cousin. "You were right, he *is* so romantic!"

Ellie returned the hug reluctantly, tears in her eyes. Yes, that he was.

* * *

It all made sense now. The second Brady caught sight of the familiar figure standing next to Ellie in the front row. His heart stopped upon seeing Claire, lovely as ever, gazing up at him with awe, or was that love, in her eyes.

But the feelings in his heart for her were nothing more than surprise. How had she known to come? Had Ellie invited her? Or, perhaps her visit was mere coincidence. Whatever the truth was, Ellie did not appear to look as happy as Claire as he took the stage.

She must be thinking that the first sight of Claire would prompt him to send Ellie packing. Brady deftly masked his disappointment with a showman's smile and began the concert. If that were the truth, how could Ellie think that? How could she take with a grain of salt everything he had told her, *especially* after all they had done together, and all she had done for him?

He had to find a way to let know Ellie know it was she whom he loved now.

The solution came to him toward the end of the show. The band performed the nearly two-hour set list with nary a mistake or flubbed line, and as Brady brought forth the band for a bow the crowd's roar was deafening. Because of the town's noise ordinance, though, they would only have time for a one-song encore. This, he knew, would have to be his chance to get to Ellie.

197

He gathered the band together for their brief break backstage, as the crowd clamored for more behind them. "Guys, there's been a change of plans," he said, and relieved the drummer and lead guitar of their duties. To Cal he said, "you think you can wing it and follow my lead for about three more minutes?"

"I'm your wingman," Cal said, and the two jogged back onstage as the crowd reached a higher octave. Brady took to the piano again; the noise in the park died as he spoke. His gaze fell to the front row; neither Claire nor Ellie had moved an inch since the show started.

"Thank you, everybody, for that warm reception." His deep voice bellowed throughout the park. "We're very glad we were able to entertain you this evening, and to help out with a great cause." More cheers. "I hope a few months from now you'll all find it in your hearts to help out with my retirement fund by purchasing my next album, which I'm working on now."

This brought more cheers from the crowd, which Brady quickly silenced by noodling on keyboard as Cal toyed with the bass. "Right now my friend Cal and I have a special treat for you. We're going to preview one of the songs from that new album. It's a song that has special meaning for me, because it's about a very special lady, from this very special town."

He glanced downward. Ellie held her poker face, while Claire clasped a hand to her heart. He swallowed, then launched into the opening notes of "Ellie."

Ellie, when I look at you...

His voice was flawless and smooth, the perfect accompaniment to Cal's impromptu bass chords. Any apprehensions he held about playing the song in public before it was ready faded as he looked out into the darkening sky. Cigarette lighters ignited all over the park during the ballad, held high by swaying fans. Encouraged, his voice grew bolder as the song progressed.

Ellie, when I lay with you...

And the images of Ellie he nursed while writing the song flashed before him. There was Ellie prancing around Jake's Market, trying to juggle a few loose apples into a bag, Ellie wobbling down a rocky dirt path on a mountain bike at some state park they frequented, Ellie curled on the sofa next to him, her head against his chest as if it has always belonged there.

There was Ellie, naked, lying seductively next to him in bed, anticipating his touch. Ellie straddled across his hips, grinding his cock into her wet pussy, her breasts swaying with each thrust, her eyelids half-closed and her lips pursed. It was all he saw now as the song drew to a close. Her voice, her moans of pleasure were all he heard and he and Cal took their final bow and exited the stage to thunderous applause.

He turned back briefly to gauge Ellie's reaction, but she and Claire were gone.

FIFTEEN

When those first words spilled forth into the microphone, Claire visibly numbed, then slowly made her way down the row. Ellie followed.

"Claire." But she could not be heard over the speakers.

Claire kept walking, pushing through people crowding the stage, until she reached the backstage checkpoint. She pushed past the bewildered young man guarding the area, ignoring his protests.

"Claire, wait!" Ellie called from behind her. She flashed her backstage pass at the boy. "She's with me," she said and dashed away before he could say anything.

She found Claire facing a short stairwell leading to the stage, her head bowed and arms folded. She was stiff as a board, and Ellie feared the first touch to her shoulder would send a searing, hateful pain throughout her body. So, Ellie approached quietly, hands at her sides. Here, the music was not so loud, so she could speak normally. "Claire," she said carefully, "I can explain everything."

"How long has this been going on?" Claire did not move.

Ellie's head lowered. "A few months. He came to town under an assumed name, to work on his new album, I guess."

"To get over me," Claire spat. "He went to Europe and it didn't work, so he comes here instead. Maybe if I had a cousin in Europe to fuck he wouldn't have come back to New York at all."

"That's not fair," Ellie protested. "You ended the relationship. It's not like we were both fooling around on you. He didn't even know who I was or that you came from here."

"Then why didn't you tell me from the start?" Claire whirled around. Ellie half expected to see eyes red from crying, or cheeks flushed with anger, but Claire's face was stone.

"I-I didn't know it was really him at first, he called himself Gary Stone," Ellie said. That much was the truth, anyway. "And when I did find out who he was, I didn't know what to tell you. I guess I couldn't decide if you would either convince me to dump him, if you believed me in the first place, or if you would come here to take him back. I didn't want you to do either of those things, because I fell in love with him."

Claire exhaled sharply through her nose, and turned back to the stage. The song was almost over, and soon Brady would descend those steps to face them both. Ellie dreaded that moment, more so than this one.

They were both silent when that time arrived, staring at each other, then at the stairwell as first Cal descended, then Brady. Cal nodded to them once and eased out of the line of fire toward a tented area where refreshments were set up. Brady approached them slowly, making his way toward

Ellie when Claire stepped into his path.

"Claire," he greeted her. "I wasn't expecting to see you here."

"Nor I you, though I've been looking for you."

"You have?" Brady's face was quizzical. Ellie felt her heart sink.

"Yes, I just want to know one thing, and I want you to be honest."

"Okay."

She saw Claire swallow, then exhale. "Do you love my cousin?" she asked.

Brady did not pause or flinch. "Yes. Very much."

Ellie let go of the breath she had not realized she had been holding, yet she was still afraid to move.

Claire nodded grimly. "Then promise me you'll treat her well," she said. "She deserves that."

"Yes, she does," Brady agreed. "And you deserve somebody who will do the same. I'm sorry it can't be me."

Claire nodded again and stepped away. Ellie let her cousin take her by the shoulder and lead her a few steps away.

"I'm not coming home with you. I'm driving straight to Norfolk to try to get back to New York tonight," she whispered. "If I can't get a flight, I'll find a hotel."

"No, Claire. Stay." Ellie meant it. In Claire's current state, who knows what she might try?

"No," Claire smiled weakly. "I don't want to be in the way. And you were right again, he did decide to move on. I had my chance." She drew Ellie into a half-hug. "At least he picked a great lady to do it with."

"You're a great lady, too, Claire." This time Ellie couldn't stop the tears. "You will find somebody great."

"Yeah." But Claire did not sound so convinced, and Ellie's heart went out to her. After a silent goodbye, Claire released her hold and walked back to her rental car, head held high. Ellie remained unmoving until she felt another hand graze her shoulders. She softened as Brady's arms slid around her waist and he kissed the back of her neck.

"Everything all right?" he asked.

"Yeah." Ellie knew she sounded as dull as Claire had. Part of her wanted to be ecstatic. Brady was hers completely, yet she could not help but feel somewhat guilty. It pained her that somebody had to walk away hurt.

"Claire's a strong lady, she'll be fine," Brady assured her. "How are you?"

"I'm better, now that you're here. I hope you're not mad at me. I can explain everything…"

But Brady pressed a finger to her lips and turned her around to face him. "Tell me later," he whispered. "I'm just glad you're here, and I'll feel much better once you realize how much I love you and want to be with you."

"I do," Ellie said. "When I heard my song I definitely knew. I love you, too, and I'm sorry I ever doubted your love."

He held her close. Ellie felt the heat of his

body send her blood pounding through her own, stiffening her nipples and melting her reserve. He bent his head and nibbled her ear, sending a shock of delight right to her core.

"I want to make love with you right now," he whispered hoarsely in her ear. "I need to be inside you so badly it hurts."

Ellie giggled. "Here, in front of all these people?" All around them people milled through the park, politely keeping their distance from the intimate scene. No doubt they were waiting for Brady to join them at the hospitality tent for a post-show toast.

That would satisfy one more of her fantasies, though.

"No, I want you all to myself tonight. If you want to get kinky later on, fine, but tonight you're all mine." With that, he scooped her up and carried her past the hospitality tent to his trailer.

Ellie held his neck tightly. "You know I just realized something," she said. "I've had this thing in my car—"

Brady raised an eyebrow. "I can't wait to learn how this is relative."

"It's a plaster kit I got at a novelty shop." Ellie giggled. "I keep forgetting to bring it out. I wanted to cast you in plaster, for all time."

"Something to remember me by when I'm not around?"

"Or when you're around, who knows."

Brady chuckled. They were at the trailer now. "We'll talk about it later. Right now you're getting the real thing."

It took a few false tries to get the door open with her in his arms, and she laughed as his balanced wobbled, but as the door closed behind them the laughter subsided, replaced with some very audible moaning.

Not far away in the hospitality tent, the post-concert revelers raised their champagne glasses toward the trailer in a jubilant toast.

EPILOGUE

Cal Briscoe leaned against one pole of the tent, glass in hand, watching his best friend carry the beautiful blonde into the trailer for a private encore. A smile flickered across his lips and he downed his drink in one swallow. They looked like a couple on their honeymoon, so in love, so oblivious to the world around them. There was no doubt in Cal's mind that, though Brady's wild days were not necessarily over, they would be forever reserved for Ellie Shaw.

A pang of sadness numbed his heart as well. He wondered if he should tell Brady that he believed he was falling in love with Ellie.

When she left the cottage last night, he had confided to Brady that he would not have minded a long-term relationship with a woman like her. His friend had laughed off the sentiment. Cal was a purebred tomcat, unable to stay in one bed for so long, and to Brady the words were mere jest.

Brady's words had hurt Cal, for he meant them. True, while he had made much of his appreciation for the female form, and had taken advantage of the female forms interested in him, there was a part of him that craved stability.

He was fifty years old, though he hardly looked it. He had never married and had no children, and had no legacy beyond his name in the liner notes of a few hundred records. He had money and great friends, but a great woman with whom to share it would be better. A woman like Ellie, sexually adventurous and willing to experiment, would be well suited for him.

Cal sighed. *Ellie* suited him. He believed this before he had been invited to share their bed. Of all the women he had laid over the years, none projected Ellie's brand of sensuality. No other woman could simply look at him and send his cock to attention the way Ellie Shaw did.

The lights in the trailer dimmed. He turned away. He wanted to be in there instead of Brady, making love to Ellie. He wanted to feel her lips tighten around and pull against his hard cock. He wanted to plunge himself into her wet warmth and fill her with his come, then nestle spent against her sweating skin, never wanting to come down from such a high.

He wanted to hear from her what she told Brady that night. *I love you.*

He patted his back pocket, then rescinded his next thought. Dareville didn't seem like the kind of place where he could light a joint without everybody protesting or calling for the cops. If nobody protested, he did not feeling like sharing it, either. It was time to go home.

He plowed through the crowd in the tent. Congratulatory remarks and good wishes glanced off him, and he simply nodded and bade everybody good night. Aroused as he was feeling, none of the women milling around the tent looked worth the time to seduce, though he was certain he could have had any one of them tonight. But he did not want just anybody, and as he headed toward his rental car he could not decide whether that thought exhilarated or frightened him.

No. He would head back to Brady's, smoke some weed, and jack off to the memories of eating Ellie's pussy. Tomorrow he would finish laying down tracks with Brady and get back to New York as soon as possible and try to forget being in love.

He had his keys in hand and pressed a button on the attached remote. The headlights to his rental car flickered, and he veered to the left, passing two women. One he recognized as Lauren, the concert's coordinator. She caught his attention with a bold wave.

"You were great tonight," she called to him. "I can't thank you enough for doing this."

Cal grinned. "Just doing it for the children," he said. "Hope everything works out for your school." He tilted his head back and glanced at the woman with Lauren. Though the park was lighted with many bright lampposts, he could not see her entirely for the shadows cast by the trees. Nevertheless, she looked very familiar with her blonde hair and voluptuous figure.

"You're not leaving, are you?" Lauren said, her voice low. "The party's just getting started."

"Sorry. I'm beat." He nodded toward the trailer. "And my boss is a slave driver. He wants that album cut next week."

"Well, have a good night then." Lauren turned

with her friend toward the tent. Cal watched their retreat, his eyes fixed on the other woman's shapely bottom, which swayed precariously with each step of her heels on the grass.

"I can't believe you didn't recognize him when you were in New York, Sue," he heard Lauren tell her.

"I can't believe it, either," giggled Sue Carmichael. "I don't know what I must have been thinking."

~The End~

Be sure to catch Cal's story in
Dare Me
avaiable now!

ABOUT THE AUTHOR

Leigh Ellwood is the pen name of a writer of mysteries; the name she has chosen for the purpose of writing romance (be it chaste, sensual, or spicy) is derived from the names of two favorite entertainers (close to it, anyway—she doesn't want to give away too many secrets). She lives and writes in the sweltering South and seeks inspiration in the many people she has met and loved over the years.

Having found moderate success in writing mystery and suspense, Ellwood decided in 2004 to try her hand (and pen) at romance. TRUTH OR DARE is the first of Ellwood's erotic Dareville series.

You are welcome to visit Ellwood online at http://www.leighellwood.com.

She also welcomes comments from readers at kspatwriter@yahoo.com.

Printed in the United States
47142LVS00002B/139-969

9 781594 265112